blank

© Charles Brownson
Ocotillo Arts
2014

Library of Congress cataloging in publication data

Brownson, Charles 1945 —
    The Sea.

PS3552.R788S   813.54

    I. Title.

ISBN 978-0-9893492-2-2

blank

not blank

The Plan Of This Book

Res non verbum
— Pierre the Chanter

THE SEA

Charles Brownson

Tempe Arizona
Ocotillo Arts
2014

THE SEA

I

OPEN WATER

Much Adoo About Nothing

What for? said Bob McAdoo. In his hand he held a glass of water because he was not supposed to be drinking and when he asked what for and flung his arms wide in welcoming puzzlement the water flew out and splashed in the face of a heavy woman in pearls smoking a cigar the length and thickness of a pencil.

The water put out the cigar.

After some sputtering she rounded on Bob. What did he mean by this? What could he possibly mean? What was it possible to mean? said this angry elderly woman in a black suit and a soaked purple silk shirt and a dead cigar.

Bob's wife Karen, who was telling this story to a group of her friends at another party, a different one, afterwards, made a few amusing comments about her husband's clumsiness. She didn't like him much, and was counting on the complicity of the others, who didn't much like their husbands either.

But who was the woman? asked one of those in the group around Karen. All of them held glasses of wine which they had become very careful of, except one coffee, who was the person who had asked.

Lydia Florent, Karen said smugly, setting down the name like a bellboy with a heavy piece of luggage for which he was about to demand a large tip.

The Honorable, said Marta, one of the wine drinkers, impressed. But, she added later to another, mixed group at her regular Thursday bridge game, it's not credible. A woman who dresses like George Eliot and smokes cigars is instantly recognizable. What happened, she said confidentially, was that Bob played the naïf and treated her like an inconsequential old lady in a ridiculous outfit which didn't suit her at all. As if he didn't know his own head of department. And The Honorable fulminated rather too long without getting an apology and so found herself with no choice but to flounce out.

It was embarrassing all around, Bob said, said Karen, she said archly.

I should say so, said the man sitting closest to the fire when he heard this story some days later.

George, the man in the club chair beside him, chuckled softly and remarked that there was little a stupefied economist might say to the government's financial director who he had just doused with water, other than to be grateful it hadn't been hot coffee.

I pretended to be an art critic, Bob said, it's said.

Plenty of those around, I imagine.

I wonder why, asked Allan Floyd, sitting opposite, they invite such people as Lydia Florent to these things in the first place?

Money, of course, Allan acknowledged a week

later to a few friends who had taken their drinks outside onto the gallery terrace. It was yet another showing of new work and the crowd inside jostled and pushed in search of the oracles. Allan made a wide gesture, indicating the paintings and other objects about, implying that he would rather be sitting beside a fire somewhere else. These gallery openings were his wife's business. Allan didn't much like his wife.

You needn't know anything if you have money, remarked Allan's wife Hanna afterwards at dinner, with some acid.

Ah, said one of the guests at table with a glass of Perrier because, as she had explained, she was driving. But *you* have money, Allan.

Yes, said another. And he doesn't know anything about art, either. Who Caravaggio was perhaps. I doubt if there were any Caravaggios about that night. Money, yes. But not that much.

The Honorable Director can't tell a Caravaggio from a Mozart.

Hardly, Lydia Florent admitted amiably. Her somewhat dusty hair had recently been coiffed but there were some strands loose nevertheless. She brushed them aside.

The man sitting to the left of the no longer empty chair at the head of the table, who had mentioned Mozart, was tiddlywinking his pencil while they waited for the meeting to begin.

And why was this McAdoo there at all, Lydia? he added with annoyance as the pencil hopped onto the rug. He knows nothing and has no influence in that crowd. He is quite penniless, ironically, in view of his profession.

Well, the Secretary began with a wry smile, but got no farther.

The Hand and the Spirit

Karen McAdoo was, like an old lemon tree, a woman of few words and most of them sour. She put all her sensuality and intelligence into her pottery. Hers was a philosophy of slurried fingertips; such ideas as she had were soft, morphic, morphiotic, wobbly-legged, but somehow upright. Her affections were dry, hard, and muscular, needing a lot of pounding and folding of the earth. It was a tectonic affection. Bob was not suited to her.

Karen McAdoo was meticulous about that as in so many other things and matters: it was Bob who was not suited. Whether she were suited to Bob was unanswerable. Pointless speculation.

She disliked to speculate. She disliked categories and general principles. But, Bob would object, this much potash in the glaze has such and such an effect on the result, doesn't it?

Sometimes, she said, declining to discuss.

Karen had an unworldly Bartleby-like preference for mute particulars. Bob simply wanted to pass over. To speak not of that which we cannot speak. That was Bob the economist. When pressed he would retreat to statistics. Probably you screwed up the potash. Everyone does. But I imagine there is a strong central tendency in these things. Mute particulars. What does that mean?

I'd prefer not to say. But it does mean something?

Probably.

The pot fell. Angry with Bob, she had squeezed too hard.

Karen sighed, cut it from the bat and threw it into the slip bucket. Nine carefully weighed balls of white clay were arranged in an exactly spaced line under plastic on a nearby shelf. She took one, centered it, and began again.

Wet clay is sexually lubricated. Pulling up a cylinder and then opening it out with her thumbs, stretching it into a bowl or a jar, was so obvious as to be a cliché. Except to Bob, of course. But that was wrong. Only some of Karen's intelligence was in her fingers, in the hard muscles of her arms and wrists. The rest of it was in her belly, where the pots came from.

Bob was a hard man to like — inconsiderate, narcissistic, passive-aggressive. Forty years of marriage had taught him nothing. Nor her. But they were married for life. It was all too complicated for an irrational person whose fingers did not like to plan too far ahead.

This business with the glass of water in the museum was so typical of Bob.

He had done it on purpose, of course.

Once, when he was away at a conference of

lesser wonks, she decided to find out how it would be to throw naked. She went at it with abandon and got herself coated from armpits to knees and had had to go out into the yard naked to hose off with icy water and it was nowhere near fun.

Another pot shivered and fell. Hopeless. She put the eight remaining balls of clay into the damp box.

Lunch. She ate hers in the studio, in the kiln room. The door of the kiln was cracked open. She had fired it three days before and had not begun to unload it, and some residual heat warmed this dark winter cave hoared with clay dust and furry moss. During a firing of that old pre-electronic kiln she had to sit up with it and there was something mystical in that, something —

One end of the house was visible from where she sat, a somewhat ramshackle artist's house in one of those miniature neighborhoods in Phoenix abounding, not far from the midtown office highrises. The street side was shaded by old mulberry and olive trees now discouraged because of their asthmatic pollen and thirstiness. The sidewalks were rumpled and the yards patchy grass — no suburban desert landscaping here. Behind this comfortable 1940s façade, the house grew fingers and toes all over the lot. Covered paths led from patios and terraces attached to added rooms to the sheds and worktables of Karen's pottery. There were jars and bowls everywhere, teapots and unmatched cups and plates in rough stony brown,

gleaming reds and creamy blues and whites, un-
glazed bone-colored bisque ware in waiting rows.
Her better pieces were on display in the house
among the bohemian furniture, bookshelves, computers. It was a mystery to her why Bob consented
to live there. She supposed he did. Bob was mostly
an annoying abstraction, like her mother who was
always pestering her to go to church and have a
baby. Go to the bathroom and have a pee.

Bob the pee.

But really, what was to complain? She had a
few like-minded friends, none of them potters, and
she had a network of colleagues in the Valley, in
Tucson and Sedona, who were cheerful and un-
competitive for the most part, and were happy to
let her have a small reputation outside the acade-
my, modest sales, and the comfortable angular
friendships typical of craftsmen.

Karen piled up a small accumulation of lunch
dishes and took them to the kitchen to wash.
Through the somewhat bleared wooden casement
window above the sink, one of its leaves cranked
open to clear the house of stuffy winter air, she
could see the east end wall of her neighbor's
house. The neighbors were marginally more kempt
than the McAdoos but no one complained. The
woman next door usually kept her curtains closed
on this side against the sun, but sometimes on dark
days she would open them and then forget. Bob
didn't like to watch that. Their daughter in the other bedroom was less careful.

Bob. Why did he want to go by such an undignified name? He made good money as an accountant, asked to serve on various influentially ineffectual committees, not in anyone's eye — at least before the water glass business. But he was still the Bob of a Montana childhood where no one has a real name.

They had married at the cloudy-minded age of twenty, at the end of the various sexual and political revolutions of the 60s, as if fleeing the explosion of some apocalyptic bomb, unaware of the betrayals and defeats to come. Wrong-footed by the times, they had continued out of step since.

It might have been worse. Karen knew she had missed out, that her fingered and tendrilled rhizomic intelligence might have had a chance to spread a bit, like those funguses which show up as mushrooms, or a thousand-year-old creosote. When she felt suffocated or abused she sought out some affair of a few days or a week, a spa or sweat-house to clean herself of the pollutants in her life. There wasn't any passion in these interludes, nor any good sex either — she supposed, having no examples to go by — but she rubbed along.

Out to lunch with some friends she once remarked about this and was surprised by a lot of dreadful stories. Her own was after all, she had to admit, nothing but the same perfunctory acceptance as what kept Bob from calling himself Robert. There had been some vying around the table for the worst experience, and a lot of ebullience, and whoever had been sitting at the other tables would have gotten an earful. The spandex crowd, fortunately.

What a familiar story, said Marta contemptuously when she heard it.

Her partner played the two of spades from the widow and remarked that everyone's lives were mostly clichés.

That shouldn't stop a person from pointing it out, Marta replied.

How about some charity? said another, playing off trump.

What for?

Timeshare

Marta cleaned up the remains from her weekly bridge game. It was always a surprise how many dirty glasses, peanut dishes, napkins, salsa-smeared chip plates, pencil stubs, dog-eared cards, balled-up scraps of paper, coins, breadballs, and pleonastic garbage can be left behind by four people doing essentially nothing.

She had thought of asking Martin to stay behind, but decided she wasn't up to that.

The dishes went in with the others into the sink, the garbage was stuffed into the already stuffed can, the coins went onto the corner of the bedroom nightstand.

She glanced out of the bedroom window through drapes never closed. There was no one on the street. There never was. There was supposed to be a downtown renaissance. That never was. She would be an old lady by then and she was not about to be a crone in a four-room condo. Martin had a timeshare in San Diego, but she wasn't up to that.

The truth was, Martin was tiresome. Just not so tiresome.

Martin himself was a sort of timeshare.

She pushed the table and four chairs back into their places and swept the tile floor. There was a new chip. It was a mistake to have put in the soft Mexican tile but the dark blood color, the hummocky surface, warmed the pit of her stomach. She had painted the walls teal, an unfortunately fashionable color, to go with the floor and some nice things of Martin's. Two 17th century maps, small etchings out of a traveling salesman's guidebook he had gotten in London, contemporary woodcuts and photographs from friends, a small watercolor from an art auction he had happened on in Bisbee, another one by a woman who had taught a Mexican workshop Marta had wasted a vacation on, a big gaudy Stephen Morath with an old truck and pumpkins and a crow in the foreground against candy-rope orange mountains, and an odd painting signed Cliff Rowe he bought out of an estate lot in a Portland gallery which he had tried several times, unsuccessfully, to authenticate. Now all friends of Marta. A comfort when the card-players were gone and the night street was lifeless and the pointless drapes were open, when there was a chip in the floor and 25¢ on the bed, and the garbage skip was five floors down.

Like something of Hopper's. Martin could never afford that.

Marta smiled, comfortably crooked, pulling her still-buttoned shirt over her head as she headed for the bedroom and banged into the door frame.

That hurt. Ugly red line on her forehead in the morning.

The smile, still crooked, became a grin.

Marta was one of The People. Everyone is. There's us, the People, and everyone else, not People. They give us a name in their own language, but that's not us.

Marta's understanding of the origins of the People was a story from her childhood. Beneath the Dreadful Mountains there was a wide plain of grass and the People came out of the ground there, sprung up from the seeds of the People Tree in the Dreadful Mountains where the Old Ones are and no one goes. If you go looking for the Old Ones you won't find them, no more than to capture wind in a bottle, but they will find you. The People Tree grows on a mesa deep in the mountains, and there is a Man Of Parts who is always trying to climb to the top but the farther he climbs the farther away he goes and what with parts of him falling off by the time he gets to the bottom there's nothing left of him and he has to start over. Once every million years the People Tree blooms and then the Old

Ones blow the seeds away onto the grassy plain
where they sprout into very tiny people like miniature Men Of Parts who are always trying to climb
up to where the Tree grows except they fall apart
before get halfway in the wrong direction. Hosts of
little People spring up from the parts and the People are like bugs in the grass and if you could get
to the Dreadful Mountains you would hear the Old
Ones laughing like the wind but you can't.

It wasn't much of a story. Children can't make
up long complicated stories. Children haven't read
Jung or the Bhagavad Gita or looked into Stith-
Thompson or studied anything at all. Their stories
just go around and around like a mad porcupine
throwing off little stickers everywhere that get into
your skin like cactus fur and you can't get them
out.

Most grown-ups can't make up stories, either,
much less long complicated ones, only the little
short ones which are lies.

It's hard to know what to do with people like
that. Marta shook her head in such a way as to
make something fall out of her ear.

Now after thirty years Marta had become an old
woman living in a condo only now it was eight
rooms and there were people on the street at night,
and coffee shops open until two a.m. and football
fans from Nebraska, of all places.

Marta was cleaning up after another bridge
game. It was the same as always — dirty glasses,

peanut dishes and plates smeared with salsa and breadballs, and still only 25¢.

With the cost of living it should be $2.50.

If she'd invested all those loose quarters and dimes at 6% she'd have $500 now, maybe. A month's grocery bill.

Martin was still around, too, though worth somewhat less than his initial offering.

Crones, however, were doing well. If she kept in shape, kept her teeth, had a little surgery for hooked nose, hormones to do something about her beard, and kept off the cane she could look forward to another twenty years of investment-grade life.

He'd kept the timeshare. They went there every year, and had crawled up the priority list to the top and now had the prime weeks in August and September when they most needed a break from the desert heat. That was the essence of a timeshare, wasn't it? The same thing at intervals forever? The puzzling part was the share. Marta had never once laid eyes on the other owners, though the preceding residents had stayed as ghostly presences. The arrangement of the crockery, dried flowers left behind, a discreet forbidden dog — probably a very faded lapdog the size of a squirrel — the oceanside sliding doors bleared above the reach of a woman about five feet two inches too lazy or unsteady to use a ladder, and no trace of a man unless he were more discreet than the dog, very unlikely.

They shared nothing with these people — this

person, beyond an aura, an effluvia. It was like sharing a candy bar with your big sister away at college, putting half of it in the care package your mom sent whenever her bridge partners asked a little too often. That was before video chat, thank god.

Her sister was more in Marta's mind now than she had been when she was alive. She'd died at 59, Marta's age, of breast cancer after she'd stressed out over an ex-lover turned stalker. Marta had had one of those herself, for a few months, until she shot him in the knee, one of the benefits of Arizona's gun laws.

Marta had never got on well with her sister, hence the stingy half a bar of chocolate gone hoary. Marta was a late mistake. Very late. Things were better now that timeshare was sold off.

In school her teachers had called her spunky, an antique word which finally got annoying. She and some girls put their heads together in the shower after field hockey. Spunk. Stuff that leaked out, so you had to wash your underwear.

What a lot of rubble had collected in her mind over the years, Marta thought as she began to wash up. First the wine glasses. Hot water. She stared at the tiles behind the sink and thought about a hot bath after. Perhaps a bit of marsala.

The People.

Twenty-five cents, the Man of Parts, sisters, dogs, Martin, spunk —

Enough to make some people weep with frustration.

Oh, yes — and that time share. It was getting on for Memorial Day. Time to make a list.

Forgotten

Martin had forgotten the teapot. There was supposed to be one and he had forgotten that the previous occupants always made off with it. Vexed, he drummed his fingers on the window sill. The window was as wide as the sea, uncovered because there was no one on that side to overlook it. Headlands, just visible on either side, enclosed the beach. The sea was wide and the sill narrow and Martin had forgotten the teapot. Marta had already left Phoenix in the Miata. He would have to go into Encinitas. Tomorrow. Go to breakfast at that restaurant with the horrible inedible fried oatmeal pancakes.

Martin once tried to eat one of these. That was when he was entitled to only two weeks in February. It was because of the pancakes that he kept going back. There was something comfortable about the restaurant's authentic loyalty to inedible food.

Encinitas he thought crass and trendy. He wished, he said to Marta, that he had bought something farther north. Carpentaria perhaps.

But he hadn't. Marta said she thought he would have made a better priest than a corporate lawyer.

The law is also a ritual, he replied defensively,

and left off drumming his fingers on the sill and
went to make a shopping list for tomorrow.

Irony

Everywhere there are people who leave their windows open. Motives vary. Some live in the country
and don't see the point of hiding what there is no
one to see, while others hide themselves because
there might be someone. Some live high enough to
be unseeable or low enough to be invisible. Still
others do it out of laziness, or forgetfulness, because they are hurried for work or impatient for
bed, or as a bohemian challenge, surly or ironic, to
the morals of their bourgeois neighbors.
    Irony is a little-understood and so often mis-
used word. It is irony when the words are not in
agreement with the facts, but if this is not deliber-
ate it is merely ignorance. Irony pretends to deny
the truth; if it should prove not a pretense then it is
a lie. A base lie, we used to say, at a time when we
thought truth was something light and ethereal
which would float away if untethered. An irony is
not a surprise, though recognition of the ironist's
real meaning may be. Willfully obscure, surprise
withheld, it is malicious. Nor is it something in-
congruous, unexpected, or not as predicted. It is a
figure of speech, of rhetoric, not a neutral statement about the nature of events or things. So when
an unobscured view of another's life is called ironic what is meant is that the exposed person's sup-

posedly bohemian challenge is in fact a compliance with the middle-class values it purports to reject. Why one should purport to untethered truth, exposing bourgeois bad faith while seeking it for oneself, is a mystery which the voyeur is not likely to look into.

Karen McAdoo, not especially bourgeois, had never encountered an exhibitionist. Bob, eating his dinner standing up at the kitchen sink, was of course blind to the whole thing despite his direct gaze. Karen had assumed that, as the intended object, his obtuseness would be a frustration, a denial of the exhibitionist's existential claim, like Schrödinger's cat which is neither dead nor alive, in fact not a cat until someone looks at it.

What was on offer was actually no more prurient than a Bonnard painting. When she was home, infrequently, the young woman in the adjoining bedroom was more forthcoming, but her narcissism was so obvious there could be no bond with the voyeur whose existence she denied. So among the three of them — mother, daughter, and neighbor — what purported to be reality was in fact illusion.

Karen herself was another matter. Afflicted with an unfashionable existential angst, nevertheless she could not bring herself to move close enough to the kitchen window to add that last bit of matter needed to cause the primal black hole to explode and create the universe again. So her lonely apotheosis accomplished nothing, and she returned to the studio to superintend a bisque firing in progress.

Mona In the Morning

Mona Magdalena's gallery Sisters was now closed to legs traffic, and her downtown presence in Scottsdale was over. Ashley had gone over to someone else on the Coast. Gordon had stayed on as her PA to manage the website and keep the books. He was gradually taking over the contacts list and would soon be selling cowboy paintings and schlock Remingtons to tourists in town for some football game, or deep-pocketed owners of Fiesta or Super Bowl boxes. The sort of people like her neighbors who would rather spend their money on a prestigious address than the symphony or investment-grade art.

Mona's husband had financed her first gallery. Looking back on thirty-five years she now saw the early 80s were the high point of the Scottsdale art scene. Those were the years of the Thursday Art Walks. Snowbirds and locals filled the restaurants in Old Town and crowded each other into the traffic on Marshall Way and 5th Avenue, and just across Indian School on 1st. Mona laid on wine and petit-fours outside and a full bar in the gallery.

That faded. Places closed, the bookshop died, the poetry readings vanished. The art scene moved on to Roosevelt Row and the invention of First Friday, a more raucous affair of young daubers, street fairs, and open studios. Bad art drives out good, Mona though sourly. She stirred her coffee, pulled her robe tight, and resented being an old curmudgeon. Some new art moved into the even newer SMOCA and the other part into the co-op galleries. Those that were left — Lisa Sette, Agnese Udinotti, Bentley Project — seemed to do well enough… she supposed…

The truth was, Mona was tired. She had been on her own for twenty years after Donald died. It had, after all, been a good run. She had done well by the money, kept the rambling old house in Cave Creek, a log and licorice-colored clapboard cave nearly as old as the village itself.

Mona Magdalena, still stirring her morning coffee until it had gone cold, sighed and smiled softly, pulled her robe tight again, and stood up to go and e-mail Gordon what to do about that pest McAdoo.

The Wanderer

After George, Allan, and the others had left the club room of the Scottsdale Resort one remained. This was Dido Makros, a morose man who had made only one remark all evening, which was to agree that Bob McAdoo had embarrassed himself, a characteristic thing for Dido to say. He was always nervous for himself of just that.

Dido's given name was Theodore, but no one had called him that since prep school. The boy had much disliked school, and the man recollected it with a shudder. He recollected it often, as the epitome and apogee of formal, institutionalized brutality — not anything which could be set down in a complaint, such as buggering by the masters or bullying from the boys, but the relentless manias, demands for conformity, and lust for physical contact which threatened Dido's shyness and made often fatal demands on his meager social skills.

Nevertheless, Dido had made enough of himself to be comfortably acceptable to a group of wealthy men chatting by a fire in the club room of a coveted resort, his habitual silence unremarked on and his eccentricities ignored. Dido was realistic enough to know that these boons were bought with money, not awarded out of kindness. Kindness is a hedge fund like any other, from which the investor expects more in return than the amount risked.

In times past, Dido reflected, he should have stayed on to finish a good cigar, rather larger than those Lydia Florent affected. In times to come, he supposed, there will be no fireplaces from the intolerable polluting smoke. Dido was of an age to regret the old pleasures without being able to adopt the new replacements, which had something to do with his moroseness.

Just now he was having a spiritual crisis. It had been coming on for a while. He was yet to discover any guru or sacred writing to help. As usual, he was on his own — for the friends who had just left him to take on a guru would be one eccentricity too many. Dido delicately rolled the ash from his imaginary cigar and stared at the temporarily real flames.

The discussion of McAdoo's gaffe in La Magdalena's reminded Dido that these attitudes were not confined to the things he knew best. He was familiar enough with the necessity of passing for what he was not, of the tugging of forelocks —

I am a Jew. Hath not a Jew eyes? Hath not a Jew hands? If you prick us, do we not bleed? If you tickle us, do we not laugh? If you poison us, do we not die?

It was something remembered from school. Something he was branded with, like boys used to be stood up on the burning deck, because out of the endless cruel sea this bit of Shakespeare had seemed to the boy his particular bit of flotsam from some unimaginable long-past wreck.

He was not a Jew, only taken for one. He was not anything.

And if you wrong us, do we not revenge? If we are like you in the rest, we will resemble you in that.

No.

He was tired of pretending to resemble. But how could he come out as something when he was nothing? How could he stand up in a board meeting, how could he say to his friends and relatives if he had any, to his imaginary wife and hypothetical children — I do not exist. You don't see me. I am not there. And go off as a sadhu in a breechclout or whatever it is sadhus wear in search of his non-existence?

The claim that he did not exist was likely as false as the claim that he did.

Excuse me.

Dido blinked and emerged from his reverie.

Someone overhead somewhere cleared his throat and asked again to be excused.

A waiter.

May I bring you another drink, sir?

Ah, Dido said in a rough, unused voice. No, thank you. I'm done for the evening. What do I owe you?

Mr. Makros has taken care of that, sir.

Has he. Well, this is for you, then.

Dido took two bills from a crumpled stash in an outer pocket of his tuxedo. The waiter took them, returned thanks, and glided away.

It was something to do with the carpet, Dido thought, that made the staff seem to move so oddly.

Apparently, Dido thought, I do exist. I paid the bill. What else, I wonder.

So. That's done.

But he was not in fact done. Dido slipped on his overcoat, a black leather duster, and walked through the lobby out onto the reception portico, where a doorman offered to retrieve his car. The car arrived, Dido got in. It was too warm. He dialed the temperature down to 68° and drove out onto Scottsdale Road. The GPS asked him where he wanted to go.

Dido smiled. It was a sardonic, temporarily liberating smile.

Home, he said.

.

The Rocks

1
The Copper Star

The first warm evening that spring — it was some-time in April, he didn't pay much attention to that sort of thing — Dido Makros put the top down on the roadster and went out for a drive. He got out a raccoon coat he had inherited from his father, along with driving gloves and goggles and a blue and white cloth cap. On the switchbacks coming down off the mountain the little car hunkered down and took a hungry hold of the road.

Dido was enjoying the drive immensely, hold-ing a line exactly a tire's width from the center stripe. For an hour he pursued the amusement of driving around Camelback Mountain, like a steel ball inside a hula hoop. He stuck close to the foot where there were fewer dead ends. Above him hung the cantilevered boxes and the porticoed mansions which followed the contours of the mountain-side like strings of chewing gum. Much grander than Dido's own, lower down. On the southeastern side of the mountain windows gleamed in the moonlight. After twice around, Di-do slowed and made some forays into the upper reaches. It was early yet. Parties were going on. Small groups were out on the decks with drinks and bent elbows. Arms cocked as if about to punch each other in the stomach. Wine in crystalline flutes or an occasional bourbon. Pretending to look at the stars occluded as always by pollution. Venus only.

Dido supposed it was Venus. That would be appropriate.

Or Mars. Wasn't Mars red? Blood.

Dido himself lived in a small house dug deep into the mountain, solar powered, mostly self-sufficient, with no decks and only a glass wall to gather heat in the winter. In summer and at night it was shuttered. Venus was hidden, and Dido never gave parties.

When he grew tired of exploring Camelback he worked his way over to North Mountain, but that was boring also and he headed up to Cave Creek Road, intending to cross over to Interstate 17. He had an idea to go to Flagstaff. The Canyon. Hike in to Betatakin at dawn.

Well, perhaps not, dressed as he was.

Some other time...

This area of the Valley, the far northern townlets, was really more to his taste than Camelback. The houses were low to the ground and far apart, hidden away beneath the palo brea, closed by mesquite and prickly pear with their pads spread out like the hands of traffic cops. Stop here. Go no farther.

So why had he not chosen to live here, instead of in the city? Dido didn't understand that. It was something to do with high and low, whether it was better to keep close to the ground, to live in a burrow, or instead to lift oneself above reach and live in an aerie. It was only something to do with keeping safe. Rabbits and mice live in holes. They know nothing of the expanse of the universe. There are no others of their kind, only the tribe and the land, and no matter how far you walk there is more of it. Eagles, geese, even butterflies know better, that there is not always more of it. To a rabbit the world is wide. For an eagle it isn't. To know that is worth the risk, Dido felt. To know the truth is worth the risk of being seen, being pointed out.

Dido turned onto the Interstate. Traffic was light at this time of night. The little roadster leapt forward like a lean dog, a cat bursting on its prey, a pheasant breaking cover.

His father took him pheasant hunting once. Dido remembered also an uncle, who he never saw again. They were on their way somewhere, rangeland, to do with oil wells. A shotgun was found for him, and when the bird flew he killed it, as he was supposed to do. The cold air, displaced by the explosion, rushed back, slapping his face. The clouds were stupendous overhead and the land went on forever. As far as he could walk.

No one said anything. There were no congratulations. It's a hen, Dido's uncle remarked then for his benefit. Leave it.

Dido understood about that when he was older and knew better what it was to be well-bred.

The road had narrowed down to four lanes and

started to climb up into Black Canyon, a six per-cent grade. Dido was taking the curves at over ninety, a hundred twenty through the straight patches. At the top of the hill the car shot up over the rim and the land seemed to drop away. He slowed; the car rejoined the earth like a falling leaf. He turned off onto the Sunset Point overlook access.

The rest stop held only 18-wheelers, idling qui-etly among themselves. Dido pulled into a parking spot at the far end, away from the toilets, and turned off the ignition. It was midnight. The moon, the glowing moonstruck eye, was closed. High clouds replaced the pollution below and the stars were still covered. Venus was gone as well; at least, he had no idea where to look for it. Here the air was cold, rapacious. Dido thought of putting the top up, but instead pulled out a blanket from the bin behind the seat, covered his ears with the collar of his raccoon coat, and pushed deeper into his seat.

There was nothing to see. He fell asleep.

On the way back down, more sedate now, Dido followed another whim and turned off at Black Canyon City where there was a roadhouse. The highway cut down here and the roadhouse over-looked it by sixty feet or so. But at the top of the gravel driveway Dido stopped in the middle of the parking lot and left the engine running. The place was somewhat ramshackle, originally a small wooden building which had been added onto indiscriminately. Two men stood on the wooden porch, talking and smoking. They glanced at the now dusty roadster, at the driver dressed in a fur coat and round goggles, and turned away again. They stood partly side by side and talked over each other's shoulders, as men do, avoiding challenge. Lean, dressed identically in jeans, boots, and khaki work shirts, they smoked and talked. The flaps of their shirt pockets were unbuttoned, where cigarettes were kept, cell phones, and a small bound notebook and a stub of pencil with which to write in the notebook whatever seemed important at the time. Heavy key rings chained to their belts. Hats, but the brims curled differently, one curled up at the sides and one flat, turned down gently at the back. The talking stopped, then the smoking, and the two went back inside.

There were five trucks in the parking lot, two with dual wheels and hitches in the beds for hauling horse trailers. Inside the talk was loud, covered by that Mexican music which sounded like polkas. It had a name, that music, but Dido could not remember what it was.

He would not go in now. Perhaps on a hot afternoon sometime, with no one there, dark and cool, he would sit in a booth in the back and drink a beer.

Dido turned the roadster around in a tight circle. He looked back, one arm behind the other seat, but soon enough drifted away, gravel crunching lightly under the tires, and returned to the highway.

He was tired. The nap at Sunrise Point — was that the name? Diamond Point — Peak? — had not been enough. The roadster drifted to the left, out of its lane. Dido was having trouble keeping up speed. Now it was morning. Traffic was thickening.

Off to the right, its barracks still blaring under fifty white-hot suns but now muted just a little by a softer dawn, one of the County jails lay down behind a filigree of chain link and razor wire.

Another roadhouse, Dido muttered. Brawls, rapes, murders. And for what? When there were so many quieter, polite ways of causing havoc. Small time hoods, petty torturers who extort only betrayal and pain and leave the treasure for more subtle thieves.

As a boy, Dido had been bullied by still unformed men some of whom might be there now, driven mad by the never-sleeping light, arbitrary and random punishment for unknown infractions, sanded to dust by what passed for human warmth and love. It was one of Dido's trials that he had to listen to their grotesque threats — which had only ever amounted to scars and broken bones — until he realized that their lives had ended, while his own had just begun, and Dido's laughter put a stop to the torment.

A snarling woke him to the present danger. He had been drifting again, into the path of an oil tanker. He jerked the wheel to the right. For three-quarters of an hour after that he managed to stay in the main current of the traffic. The bustle around him grew. He felt like an uprooted tree, a snag moving slowly, causing turbulence.

And then he missed his exit, unable to reach it across two packed lanes. Dido worked his way to the right and got off at Indian School Road one intersection too far south. He turned east. The sun was in his eyes.

And then another mistake. Dido realized that he was about to run out of gas. Casting about, he saw a station on the near corner and pulled into the narrow portico between the building and two old pumps which were obviously not working. The bleary windows facing them stared in lidless stupor.

Now what? Dido backed up. Where was the exit onto the street? Hunting around behind the building, he found to his puzzlement that the place wasn't a gas station at all, but a coffee shop, like a boy in the husk of an old roué. He parked the roadster and went in. It had been twelve hours.

There were not many tables, and only one unoccupied. Dido put his cap and goggles down there to reserve it and went to the counter. To the wrong end. A genial man with a pony-tail directed him to the other end, and there took his order for coffee and a sandwich.

Room for cream?

No.

Cup or mug?

Mug.

What size?

Small. A large one gets cold before I finish.

Breakfast?

What is there?

The counter man gestured toward a board beside the register, but Dido was unable to take it in. Egg and sausage.

Wheat or sourdough?

Dido asked for a croissant and was offered a bagel, which provoked a new flood of questions about flavor, toasted, buttered, and several other things. Then it seemed there was also a choice of sausages. Salsa no. More possibilities. Dido began to laugh uncontrollably.

Just one more thing, the counterman said. What's that legendary coat?

Raccoon. It was my father's.

Grandfather's, wouldn't it be? Flappers and speakeasies and rumble seats? Not around here, though. Then.

Well, yes, Dido admitted. Probably. They lived in Philadelphia, I think. My father never said.

The counterman's round open eyes glimmered. Can I feel? he said, shyly. Dido held out his sleeve and the other man caught it between his fingers.

Awesome.

He let go. Dido withdrew his arm from over the vitrine with its scones and rolls, reluctant.

Here's your coffee. I'll call you when the sandwich is made.

Dido nodded in acknowledgement, made his

way back between the tables, and sat with his back to the wall. The other customers were all women, some seeming students with open laptops, a texting high-school girl, a woman in casual business clothes dripping butter onto a folder of papers she was marking up, a woman about Dido's age in running clothes reading the *Republic*, which she had folded up into a tight square like a veteran strap-hanger.

One of the students raised her head, saw Dido, and smiled. She closed the lid of her computer and began to collect her things into a large cloth sack.

Have a nice day, she said, and somehow meant it.

And you as well, Dido responded formally.

The counterman brought his egg and sausage sandwich on sourdough with mayonnaise and mustard and a pickle and a great deal else present or absent.

My coffee?

You wanted a mug of coffee, he said. I forgot. Not a foam cup but a mug. I'll get it. I like that coat, man.

Thank you, Dido said. Thanks for remembering about the mug.

The counterman wiped his hands on his apron and went back to get a mug, which he filled himself at the rank of coffee urns underneath the posted menu.

I guessed you wanted French roast, he said, putting down the mug delicately.

Dido took a bite of sandwich. He chewed it slowly. He chewed for days, weeks. That sandwich would never be eaten. In times to come Dido would still be there, unable to leave because his car was out of gas, with his sandwich and the teacher dribbling butter on her students' homework and the man who liked his grandfather's raccoon coat.

He would take the bus home.

Eventually.

2
The Fair Trade Cafe

He looks like Klaus, someone said.

Who does?

No, I mean a Klaus. He looks like someone named Klaus.

How is that?

I don't know — square. Tall, square, blond.

What was he before?

Downtown, a third voice spoke. Payroll.

Why do we have an engineer in Payroll?

To fix things, of course, said the first voice.

A guffaw, Klaus thought, pushing his coffee mug in a random walk around the table. One of those people who pump out a guffaw after everything they say.

It was Klaus's second day as an inspector. He was neither from downtown nor payroll, not square, and Maricopa County had not seen fit to put Air Quality on the building across the street. He was not even tall.

Gordon was amused by this story when he came, late as usual. I try to be, he said.

Try what?

You're not very tall, the girl says negligently, and Marlowe says I try to be, and pulls on his ear-lobe — Bogart does — like this.

Gordon pulled on his earlobe. It wasn't a very convincing gesture.

Klaus drank some of his coffee and made a face.

I don't like this place, he said. It's pretentious.

It's across the street. Con-vee-nient.

In the conference room with the door open, Klaus grumbled. Never thought whether I might hear. Fair Trade, it says. What's fair about it?

Well, said Gordon soothingly, it means the growers get a fair price for their coffee, set by the buyers' agreement, enough to live on. The big growers exploit them.

Everyone does, Klaus pointed out.

Spoken like a square, tall, fair payroll account-ant, Gordon said.

A Metro train slid into the station outside the window like a bar of green soap, heralded by a tin-kling and a discreet, hoarse squawk. The street door of the Fair Trade Café was propped open and the sound came in on a breeze which passed through and out the back.

Gordon was looking about for a better seat. Let's move out there, he said. In the back by the fountain.

The Fair Trade was L-shaped, fronting on two sides of a corner. Behind the building a passage ran through, with the fountain at the center of a small brick terrace.

Nice neighborhood, Klaus said as they settled into new seats. I wonder what they get for those condos up the street. The building looks empty.

More than I can afford, Gordon said, unless they stay empty. Since Mona sold the gallery I need to be up in Cave Creek anyway, or far north Scottsdale at least. I can't afford that, either.

So she should pay, Klaus said. What do you do for her? Today, I mean.

There's a co-op studio over on Grand. Mona heard of an artist working there and I was having a look. A painter.

Any good?

No.

Cartoon Mexicans, probably. Graffiti. Bazat.

Basquiat. It always surprises me what you know, Klaus, even if you're thirty years behind in this case. More than I know about engineering, certainly.

I don't like that stuff, Klaus said. His coffee was cold. He stood up to go for another.

Jasper Johns is who I like, he said when he returned. Restful. Clyfford Still. Big black canvas with a red drippy shape down one side. I never saw anything of his before that one. In San Francisco.

It was all in storage. Denver has it now. You have an odd idea of what's restful, Klaus.

No I don't.

You didn't find it unsettling? There's a tension. Anxiety.

No.

Tension and anxiety was something else. It was what Klaus felt when he was waiting for Gordon. He was always waiting. Gordon got distracted. He'd spent all his time with that painter who wasn't any good and then got himself involved with one who was worse. He just couldn't help himself. Klaus was the other way. He didn't like to waste time on people like that, people who were going nowhere, but Gordon always thought maybe they would and he might miss the bus.

Everybody thinks they're going somewhere, but they aren't.

After Gordon had left, Klaus sat on. He didn't want a tuna sandwich. In his office he had a bag lunch because he hadn't known where there would be to eat. He didn't want that, either.

Finally he went, leaving through the south end of the passage. He crossed on Roosevelt. Another train arrived. He thought about getting on it. He thought about going to Denver to see the Clyfford Stills.

In his office, Klaus retrieved his bag lunch. It was not quite noon. He walked two doors down the hall and into the office of the man who had called him square. When he stood up, Klaus punched him in the stomach.

The air went out of him in a fetid puff, followed by a dribble of vomit. He went a little cross-eyed and put one hand out to steady himself on a corner of his desk, but he missed and crumpled to the floor. Puzzlement and grief filled his eyes.

Klaus took the elevator down to the lobby and walked across the slippery-looking marble floor to the exit to the garage. They hadn't given him a number yet, so his car was parked in a visitor space in the second level. He came out of the garage on Roosevelt and made his way to 7th Avenue, where he got onto the freeway heading west. He thought maybe he would go to San Diego. He had enough gas to get to Quartzite, anyway.

What is there to do in Quartzite? Anything?

3
Steve's Espresso

Since she had restarted her degree, Ashley had quit thinking about Gordon Brisbane, Mona's factotum. Climbing little man. Climbing men are always little even if they aren't. Climbing women are something equally uncomplimentary, she thought, but couldn't find the image. Something to do with ancestors in trees. But that was a month ago. Now she was back at ASU and she had discovered this neighborhood coffee shop on Baseline across from a Chevrolet dealer and it was not a bit like Gordon

Brisbane, nor machine-made like a Starbucks either. Steve's Espresso. Until a few days before there had been some big photographs and drawings on the wall for which some climbing artist was asking $50, but now these had been replaced by comfortable old magazine illustrations, which was the sort of thing Steve liked.

She did wish Steve wouldn't play techno music. Or at least turn it down.

Steve drove a silver-blue BMW roadster. He said he used to sell medical equipment or something and the BMW was left over from that. An empty, corrupt job, Steve said, cheating sick people and stealing from the government.

Ashley, too, was now among the sick people who hoped if they paid enough they might get well. Among sick people she could make pots again. Pottery is made out of dirt and marks the line where society becomes civilized. Settled agriculturists who need something to store food in against the future. One of those really basic activities like story-telling and propitiating the gods. When archaeologists start finding broken pottery they know that the tribe has begun to live in villages and towns and cities with kings who fight wars with each other. Ashley was glad to be getting her hands dirty again and sitting in a coffee shop looking at a car dealership and listening to techno.

She had bought a bicycle to get around on, though she would have preferred a scooter, but she couldn't afford that. A Vespa like you see in Rome in swarms like — she fished her mind for a comparison. Everything which swarms is nasty. Butterflies, but they weren't a very good metaphor for two dozen squalling Vespas paying no attention to pedestrians, traffic lanes, or sidewalks.

A purple one, that's what she wanted.

Ashley looked about her at the others in the shop. In front by the window two deaf girls were signing enthusiastically, talking over each other in the way that women do. At an outside table was a woman with a dog, smoking. Inside, at the table beside her, three men were talking about the Bible and compassion, and also nearby a man with a laptop was selling insurance to a twenty-something couple who didn't need it. At the counter another college student was chatting with the barista. A woman was texting. Steve was in the back making peanut butter cookies. Up to heaven thence will I bring them down. Though they hide themselves in the mountains I will search them out. Though they flee to the bottom of the sea thence will I command the serpent and he shall bite them.

Another easy one — Revelations. The Bible readers were a little flummoxed at being talked down.

So they hid in a cave, she said, after riffling back a ways, and Joshua said roll great stones over the mouth of the cave and keep watch until they are dead, and stay you not, but pursue your enemies, and smite the hindmost of them, and they made an end of slaying them with a very great slaughter till all were consumed.

You're talking about injustice, another of the men said. It's not the same thing.

Yes, it is. Ashley snapped, suddenly very angry. What about Job, who God leans on until he gets down on his knees and bares his neck so God can smite off his head. Job had to admit that he loved God, you see, before God could compassionately smite off his head. It's out of compassion we build new prisons for drug addicts and murderers, havens where — 'scuse me.

She reached for her backpack which was still on the floor under the table she had abandoned and walked as inconspicuously out as she could, leaving behind the mug of coffee the barista had forced on her.

A ways up the street Ashley stopped pedaling and put her feet on the ground in the middle of the bike lane. She was going to get in front of a car if she didn't pay attention.

What was that all about? It was if she had been speaking in tongues.

Maybe she could ask Steve to turn down the techno music a bit.

4
The Coffee Plantation

On a warm Monday morning in April Allan Floyd was sitting in a Coffee Plantation café on the north border of Paradise Valley. It was just past 7am, far earlier than his usual time. He had left the house on Mummy Mountain without a shower, and without dressing properly, so as to be gone before his wife came out of her bedroom in search of toast and orange juice. When she was gone he would go home and start the day properly.

It was already ninety degrees. Allan was sitting near the door, and the constant stream of early seekers after coffee, bagels, and scones brought a steady chuffing of hot air. There was nowhere else to sit. He was sweating. He shucked off the poplin beige jacket which he wore and opened another button at the neck of yesterday's shirt. The pants did not go with the shirt nor the brown shoes with the pants. His ankles were naked. Very European. That was not much consolation.

Allan Floyd despised this place — a mixed clientele of community college students and petty bourgeois office workers in banks, brokerages, credit card fulfillment, and other businesses which did nothing but stir the cauldrons of money like Macbeth's three witches, listening to their predictions of coming power.

Allan Floyd despised his life — a yacky-tacky vulgar house at the end of a pompously named cul-de-sac in a town whose greatest public works were a network of speed traps and street cams to keep people from coming there. He felt cheated and bitter about it and choked on his cold coffee on an unseasonably hot morning.

A slim man with a muffin in one hand and a styrofoam cup in the other and a leather bag on a shoulder strap was standing at the end of the table. Allan floated to the surface of his reverie.

Excuse me, the slim man said. Would you mind if I sat here? There's nowhere else.

Allan gestured negligently toward the empty chair on the other side of the table. The man took possession of it, putting down things one by one — the coffee, the muffin, the bag, and out of his jacket pockets a phone and a little notebook and a silver pen and lastly a copy of a novel by Donna Leon. Couldn't find my Kindle, he said apologetically. Allan pulled his hands and his coffee cup back into a corner of the table in self-defense at this onslaught of stuff. Keys, a wallet, a card case, another phone, a pair of reading glasses. Out of the bag came file folders, a tablet, two more pens, and a wad of receipts. It was comical. Allan felt his sour mood lift. He noticed that this man, too, wore no socks.

The fellow took a sip of coffee and gazed at his small hill of trinkets, both amused and puzzled. One of the phones sang out, He winkled it out of the pile, looked at the caller ID, and smothered it.

Ah! he said suddenly, and plunged one hand into a side pocket of his bag. From there he took a small, round, blue pill case. The lid he dialed to Monday's compartment, from which he turned out three small pills into the palm of his other hand. He took them dry. Then, satisfied and at peace, he began to put everything back.

Fastidiously, Allan polished a bit of the newly uncovered table with a paper napkin. The younger man began a breathless apology, broke off to gulp down some coffee, grabbed his bag and fled, leaving the untouched muffin.

Allan eyed this muffin for a while like a suspicious prairie dog. Surreptitiously he drew it toward him by a corner of the napkin on which it lay. After another long side-eyed stare he broke off a piece. This crumb lay on the table for a while until he ventured a nibble. Slowly his anger and bitterness returned and he pushed the muffin aside. It was too sweet.

He had had a row with Hanna the previous morning. This was no great matter — morning rows were common — but that one had been fierce and he didn't want another. She was beavering away at some academic paper she was writing, coming home past midnight, and it made her cranky. At the time when their children were still at home this had been a daily occurrence, leaving Allan to scratch together clothes and food. Alicia boiled spaghetti, Daniel fried some hamburger, and the little one unscrewed the top from a bottle of catsup and dribbled it on the floor. They had made do.

Now that had started again. One Domenic Parra, whose dissertation she was supervising, would find her out and it would be after midnight getting home. Something to do with Buddhist mudras.

Hindu mudras. Allan didn't ask. Degrees in art history and comparative religion were not on-putting. On trips she always wanted to visit every cathedral and church and stare at ceilings. On their first trip to Florence he had adjourned to an espresso bar and hadn't been in a cathedral since.

And he did know what a mudra was. And that Donna Leon wrote stories about Venice.

Hannah had always been contemptuous of what he knew, as if people who inherited money and didn't work at something were bound to be buck-ignorant. Hanna didn't see that what he did was work. Up long hours at night at his computers, no office or IRA, no mailroom or coffeemaker or photocopier. But he went on stirring his cauldron anyway and out of it came more noxious money. He had started with a few bats' wings and mice hearts and now Hanna drove to work in a natty Mercedes, always new, and wore things she said were ostentatious to gallery openings and to the opera whenever they were somewhere with a decent opera house, and wore ostentatious jeans to work.

Allan felt exploited. He did not think that unnatural, if she used his money to finance research trips to Europe and Asia instead of struggling with grants, money which had bought her tenure and a department chair in a second-rate university and big roles in professional societies with cauldrons. She had squeezed three children out of him and herself, all three of them liberal ideologues who had nothing to say to people who do nothing useful, and after the third one she wondered why he preferred to make money at night.

Despite that, she kept herself fit. She found time to go running most mornings and was scrupulous about what she ate. It made Allan angry that she would concoct crude, ludicrous scenarios because she believed him incapable of doing likewise, indeed of anything subtle or reasoned. So every morning he buttoned up, maliciously left the orange juice on the breakfast table to warm, and like some stupider Othello went out to the Coffee Plantation on Shea Boulevard to drink his cup of bitterness and resentment, black, no room. Though usually not so early as this, and usually with his socks on.

Allan Floyd went home again. The nifty evernew Mercedes was still parked at its usual rackety angle in the driveway and the orange juice was warm. Her crumpled valise stood, or leaned, on the hall guest table. Allan never found anything interesting in it. He looked at her calendar and saw that, as he thought, she had missed her morning lecture. Cautiously, he put his ear to her bedroom door. Nothing.

He went away to do some work. After lunch things had not changed, so he put on a brazen face and rudely opened her door.

Hanna was lying across the still-made bed wearing only a bra. Allan noticed with interest that she was going bald between the legs. After a while some men came and bustled her away.

He never found out what happened. The high point of the day turned out to be the breathless man who had misplaced his pill case.

5
Mama Java's

Fedya Volkoff was reading some of his poems at Mama Java's on Indian School and 36th. There were eight people, six of whom weren't really listening and seemed to be from Montana. Fedya was not good at patter. Between poems he shuffled papers and listened to what they were saying. Two of them had just come in from the antique shop on the corner of the strip where they had bought some Indian pottery which they now unwrapped.

Is this genuine? the oldest of the three men asked suspiciously.

Of course. See here.

A sort of consultation began which Fedya could not understand. In the middle of his next poem a rather louder remark about the unlikely genuineness of anything to do with Indians put Fedya off his rhythm and he had to step back two lines. Not long after they wrapped up the pottery again in crumpled paper and two plastic grocery bags and went out.

The remaining two were a couple he recognized from other readings. The man was soft-spoken, with a short ginger beard and wearing a black, narrow-brimmed hat of a sort Fedya did not know, of

a height in between a pork-pie and a top hat. The
woman never spoke at all. She wore a heavy green
skirt in several layers and a short green jacket to
match, with her black hair in a single thick braid,
the whole a generic Andean peasant outfit. She
moved extremely slowly, as if the air here, below
15,000 feet, were wearyingly congealed. She was
eating a biscotti, which she dipped into her coffee
at one spot, then changed her mind and tried another. Finding the right spot, she melted off the
wet end in her mouth and then embarked again on
another aesthetic expedition.

His poems were heaped untidily on the seat of a
blond wooden bad stool. As he shuffled through
them the door of the coffee shop opened and his
friend Domenic came in, along with a woman in
her sixties with short salt-flecked hair dressed in
casual clothes with ironed-in wrinkles. Domenic
smiled, stopped to say hello, then went to the bar
to get coffee. Fedya advanced to a new slide on his
laptop which was sitting on a second barstool. The
image was of a volcano erupting with smoke.

      With a click the mood changes.
      New window, morning breeze.

A faint hiss from the slow-moving woman in the
heavy green shirt suggested some disapproval, but
Domenic's companion smiled transparently, just a
slight recurve of her mouth. He felt awkward and
disorganized, and the long silences between po-

ems, which should have been filled with clever
remarks and reminiscences preferably not apropos,
made the performance all the more lame.

Two more couples came in and found tables,
then moved to the sofa in the conversation area on
the other side of the room. Almost immediately
one of the men went to sit outside and smoke.
Fedya began to relax.

A new knife does not cut
fibers like worms
but slips between them
quantum-oiled,
separating them like a lover
through a marriage.

Feeling he'd put a foot wrong with that one,
Fedya's relaxation vanished. He abandoned that
poem and began another.

The two women who had just come in were
sharing the sofa uncomfortably. One of them
laughed at Fedya's poem, a short bark, and hooked
a nearby hard chair with her foot to use and an ot-
toman. The non-smoking man came back with lat-
tes, a chai, and two cookies. The smoker came in.
Standing behind the sofa, eating a cookie, he waited. They all waited, eight of them, for Fedya.

Now that you're all here, he said, drawing a little laugh, I'd like to read something different, a
longer poem entitled "The River Derwent".

She'd heard the old mission had been restored
recently, put back into place
so to speak, its grubby old age
wiped off like a fogged mirror Jake would say,
and had come to see for herself.

Fedya had never read a long poem. Before this
one, he had never written a long poem. As the
words went on he began to worry about droning, or
worse, delivering it in that awful poetry voice with
its deathly hush and falling cadences. Profound in-
sights spoken here.

Finished reading, he felt a little hoarse and went
to the bar for a glass of water. Domenic approached from behind, and when Fedya turned,
took his hand and shook it warmly.

A good poem, he said. Keep it.

Fedya wiped his other hand, wet from the glass
of ice water, across the front of his shirt. The four
people in back went out laughing. The ginger-
bearded man in the short hat stopped to say to
Fedya that he'd enjoyed it and went out also with
the somnolent green peasant, their twined fingers
locked.

The woman Domenic had come with now
walked over to the coffee bar. She was short, not
much over five feet, tough and spare. She stood a
little forward, on the balls of her feet. A spring-
wound terrier.

You see, she said, in a quiet musical voice
which belied her appearance, your advertising

wasn't all for naught.

Yes, I do see, he said. But he didn't.

You are better poet than I expected, she added, and turned to go. Seeing that, Domenic turned also. He held the door open, went through politely after, a man a foot taller and half-again her weight, but by comparison soft and tentative.

Then Fedya knew who she was — Domenic's professor about whom he was in constant despair, sitting at the kitchen table in Fedya's apartment with his head in his hands, fretting over missed references and endless revisions and overlooked sources.

It's never good enough, he said in a muffled voice. I'll never be done with it.

Domenic raised his head and made a gesture with his right hand, which he stared at in disbelief.

Hmp, he said, and made a different one.

Hmp. He put his hand out and shook it as if shaking off some dirt. She teaches medieval church architecture, Dominic complained. What does she know about Buddhist mudras?

His mind emptied by the reading, Fedya went about shutting down his laptop and gathering his poems. Half the sheets had fallen in the floor. A sheaf of them was crumpled into a baton in his fist. For a long time he stood quite still, as if about to direct his audience in some music, a march perhaps, but with his head turned right around, almost over his shoulder, to the door.

A boy rode up on an old bicycle which he

leaned against one of the outdoor tables.

Oh, he said, coming in. It's over.

And he turned and rode away again.

6

The Xtreme Bean

Lindsey sat by herself as usual. Her three suite-mates crowded together on the other side of the table speaking in intense low voices masked by the hubbub in the coffee shop. It was always this way. Lindsey tagged along. She sat outside the light, not hearing, waiting. To go home, or not go home, left behind by other friends, boys, not boys.

They were here. Someone had said go there, we'll see you there. The Xtreme Bean. Southern and McClintock. Used to be a bank. It looks like a bank. Tonight.

Monday night. Why? No one told her to go there, said they'd see her there. The coffee shop or the library, alone either way. So Lindsey sat at the vacant end of the table with her latté, waiting for whoever it was who had told them to come here to show up and leave her to take the bus home.

Lindsey had never been here before. It was, after all, still September. She had had only a month to learn the bus routes. Her suite-mates had three cars among them, a Lexus and two Hondas, all new. Someone had said, go there, we'll see you there, so they went, and saw them, and Lindsey tagged along. Probably one or two would bring friends home and there would be sex on the common area sofa because the beds hadn't been made or something, with a lot of grunting and screaming which blocked the path to the kitchen. Lindsey would want some cheese and crackers, or something else, always something, and didn't want to go and get it because of the sex. It was squalid. She was sure the girls were faking it and would take care of themselves later. Why did they bother?

It was Monday. A sign on the door said that on Mondays someone played old-time piano from seven to nine, and there was a piano in the corner, opposite the vault, and a tallish, thin man with a mop of gray hair was sitting on the stool with a pile of sheet music on another stool beside him. He pulled something out of the pile and smoothed it onto the rack and began to play. He had a flat-fingered style, a no-energy way of working the keyboard, sliding down and back, passing his hands over the keys as if about to produce a colored scarf or a smear of playing cards.

He started with some barrelhouse tunes, Fats Waller, Doctor John, but played softly, almost introspectively, and went on to some meditative blues. The notes didn't exactly cry. They commiserated. He made no announcements. Lindsey recognized the music as what her grandfather had played, the records a little scratchy, wearing out. Her grandfather was — had been — not so old time as that, as this piano player with the curly gray hair resting with folded wings oh his ears.

There was a break. Lindsey turned around in her chair, reaching for her latté, and found that the others had gone, leaving her without a word. The drink was cold. Lindsey wrinkled her nose. The pianist was starting on some show tunes from the 1940s. As Time Goes By, Hoagy Carmichael stuff from early television, and then, abruptly, The Maple Leaf Rag, as if giving in to demand, but nobody was demanding anything. One boy sitting by the wall with his laptop open, his face inches from the screen, was tapping his foot. Most of the tables were occupied, but it didn't seem as if anyone was listening.

Lindsey got up and moved closer, to a club chair at the old man's back. After two more tunes he turned on his stool and said hello.

She nodded in reply, started to speak and then retreated.

You heard this music before?

Lindsey nodded again. My grandfather, she said.

He was a piano player?

Just records.

Where was this?

All over. You know.

What you doing here, then?

It's a big place. I wanted to go to a big place.

From where?

I like not being noticed.

By such as me, eh?

This seemed to be the end of the exchange, for the old man turned back to the piano and began to play again. This time it was a little different, a hesitating tune with thick chords, interspersed runs and arpeggios that seemed always about to end but never did.

That wasn't so old, Lindsey said when in fact the music did stop.

You think. Nineteen forty-four.

I heard it before.

Sure you did. Monk played it in the sixties, when you were about minus thirty.

What is it? Lindsey asked.

Round Midnight. Look — he hesitated.

Lindsey.

Lindsey, I want to have a smoke. Come and sit with me out there.

He nodded toward a covered passage where some rickety bistro tables had been set up.

My name's Huck, he said when the cigarette was burning. Called me that all my life. Don't know why.

Where are you from, then?

Minneapolis. Too cold. There and around Chicago, then up and down the coast a few years. Wears a man out, that. Got to settle down.

Why here? Lindsey asked, her shyness melting.

It's a big place, he said.

No it isn't. Or it wasn't, anyway. And what about Los Angeles?

I got tired of that, Huck said quietly, scraping

the ash from his cigarette, rubbing it to a point on the metal meshwork of the table top. Little sparks fell on the concrete at her feet.

What happened to your friends? Huck asked, changing the subject.

They left. Do you get paid here? Lindsey asked, changing it back.

Here? No. It's for fun, here. Messes up my taxes if I get paid for playing here.

You're retired then. Huck, she added, hesitantly.

Retired. Huh. Yes, I guess that's what I am.

But you play.

I do. Yes, I do. Lindsey, are you going back to there when you're done here?

No. There's nothing for me to do there.

What did you have in mind? Huck asked. He lit another cigarette.

I don't know. It's too early to tell.

You're not good with your friends, I think, Lindsey.

No, she admitted, startled at this turn. I'm moving out after the semester. They're from California. Los Angeles somewhere.

A lot of people are from Los Angeles, Huck said quietly, as if that were too big a bucket not to have some water in the mud.

I don't know. One of those places along the coast. Encinitas, Ventura.

You're geography's not too good.

No, she admitted, and the anger toward her

suite-mates which had been building now drifted away on the curls of smoke. Are you going back to play, then? Huck?

Play. Yes. Yes, I am.

I'm going to find a bus, Lindsey said.

The 81, catty-corner on McClintock.

Oh. Thanks.

Lindsey and Huck shook hands, and Lindsey went around the outside of the Xtreme Bean, across the parking lot past the Walgreens and the closed Basha's grocery and two sides of the intersection to the bus stop. Behind the stop was a place selling Middle Eastern food to go. Her stomach tightened with hunger — there had been only the latté since lunch — but at home there were crackers and hummus which was going to spoil, unless the other girls had eaten it already. Lindsey doubted that.

Huck, she repeated to herself. The 81 bus came, and she got on, showing her student pass. There was no one else on the bus. She sat down in the second row behind the driver and watched the night-lit city pass by, and the edges of the University, a Metro train, the transit stop. She got off there, and walked home.

7
The Coffee Lab

Listen to this, someone was heard to say. I'm taking this class on Quine and we have to do this paper, so here's the paper.

I perceive, said the rat to the mole, that your tunnels do not go straight.

I perceive, said the snake, that you do not run straight.

I perceive, said the mole, nothing.

There is nothing, said the snake, swallowing.

I perceive, said the badger, a snake.

Chas looked about for the speaker. The Coffee Lab was a small place and the philosopher-poet was not hard to find. The fellow sitting with him was writing desultorily on a scrap he tore from his notebook.

Well, I don't think you're going to get top marks, Dugan, he said.

Au contraire, mon ami. C'est exactement les préférances du Professeur .

What exactly is this an argument for? said Dugan's friend after considering what he had written on the scrap.

Ah. Quine, as you know, objected to synthetic truths.

That's not right, said the other, and began to bounce his pencil on its eraser. It was the distinction between synthetic and analytic.

Yes, yes — but if you take away the distinction the categories evaporate, don't they? So the idea is, experience validates —

Or not.

Validates our beliefs not severally but in their entirety, Dugan said. You can't logically separate individual ideas from each other, any more than a single perception. They come in packages. If you want to disbelieve —

All right, OK, so this, um… what the hell is this thing, anyway, Dugan? A koan?

It's a paper, dude. Rat makes an observation about the relationship of experience to expectation —

What happened to rat, by the way? I was just getting interested in him and then we don't hear any more about him.

It's not a novel, man. It's a paper. An argument.

This is a paper, the skeptic said, holding up the scrap.

In the dark, one table over, Chas couldn't make out whether there was anything written on it at all.

The student of Quine made an impatient noise. It's a piece of paper.

Hey, said the other. That's what Quine meant, isn't it? About this dialectic of experience and belief?

Fuck, said Dugan, disgusted.

I don't know, man. Maybe it's worth some kind of grade after all. But there's no documentation. Where are the footnotes?

Footnotes, dude? On a koan?

Ah ha. The skeptic pounced, pointing the eraser end of his pencil at his friend. Ah ha.

Chas went to the bar for another cup of coffee.

While his back was turned, Dugan and his friend slipped out, snagging Chas's flash drive which had been lying on the table next to his laptop. The computer's little green light glowed in the dark, marking the whereabouts of the livid slab. There hadn't been anything on the flash drive except some pictures of his girlfriend.

The pictures turned up on Facebook by the end of the day. There was a flurry of text messages between them.

They stole my flash drive, I told you, he wrote again.

Right. How does this look when I apply for a job?

So Chas did a little work. He found the listing for the Quine course and got Dugan's last name, and then his address, and soon Chas had a fairly complete profile. It was dull stuff. Chas walked his cursor through the words on his laptop screen, thinking of what to do.

Let the punishment fit the crime. Appropriate, proportional. Eats away at the rule of law otherwise. Socially destructive, but not outside expectation. First the punishment, then the crime. What is the crime? Kafka.

Chas discovered that he was bouncing a pencil on its eraser end. A pencil? Why did he even have a pencil?

Because when they set the table for meetings they put down a glass for water, a pad of yellow paper, and a pencil. He had walked off with the pencil.

The crime. Dugan the bailiff delivers the punishment. Judgment of the court. Some notion of fit and proportional. Mystical arithmetic preserves social coherence.

In a few days the students' latest papers had been marked. Dugan had been given a C. The slacker's grade.

Experience suggests that existence is governed neither by justice or power but some sort of arbitrary — Chas found himself browsing the whole catalog of 20th century metaphysical anxieties. He left a message for his former girlfriend. There was no reply. He could have hacked Dugan's grade to a D, or — what would have been odder — a B, but he doubted he had the skill to keep his fingerprints off that. Besides, there was a pile of personnel decisions which needed vetting, mostly reassignments and downsizes. Attaching his cursor to the tab, Chas pulled the pile forward and began to work through them.

8
Essence Bakery and Cafe

Hanna Floyd had gone for breakfast to Essence, a coffee shop on the corner of University and Hardy, because she had been told that it was one of three in the Valley to make authentic croissants. They did, but the place was not a coffee shop but a café. The coffee urns were in the back, and empty. The place was tiny. It was also jammed and impossibly noisy. Hanna ate her croissant and abandoned any idea of a leisurely half hour reading a detective novel she had found on the $1 table in a used book store, formerly (it said on the flyleaf) the property of someone illegible, possibly Bob Crotchet. On the laptop unremoved from her valise, a Mac thinner than two dimes, were unmarked student papers and citations to a dozen professional articles which she hadn't retrieved from the library's myrmidon e-journals. Out of the question. As if she had ever wanted to read those things for breakfast anyway.

She spied a free table outside among the smokers and carried her things there — the empty coffee urns had been refilled at last — just beating out a haughtily-dressed pair of women who had not ordered anything.

There's a table inside, I think, Hanna said with a pretense of helpfulness, knowing neither would hear a word the other said. So much for networking. Sour faces and fled in a gray Audi. The parking lot, Hanna saw now, was full of such cars — BMWs and Mercedes like her own, black or white, striped Mini-Coopers, Lexi, even a red 1955 Corvette with the top down which she had seen before and wondered how anyone dared take it out of the garage.

On this corner were also a Sacks sandwiches, an Ethiopian restaurant, a Papa John's pizza, and a drive-through Starbucks. Across the street a Rosita's Mexican food and a Cornish Pasty. And up half a block in the direction of the freeway was a feed and tack which was there long before all this, or any freeways at all.

It was Domenic who mentioned this place. Hanna occasionally taught on the other campuses, West, Downtown, Polytechnic — Polytechnic was a food desert. More or less nearby in Queen Creek was said to be a charmless but decent Mexican relic older than Tempe Feed and Tack patronized by Hispanic laborers from the days of Tubac presidio. In Gilbert there was a hamburger place with lines out the door and electronic buzzers to announce when your food was ready. The only good thing about that place was a picnic table outside under an incredible banyan-like tree with lower limbs propped up on 4x4s and a massive trunk which looked to be made of ropes of taffy and was probably as old as the Yaquis.

Allan thought she was having an affair with Domenic. Allan was a stupid man whose only talent was making money and it suited her to instill a little jealousy in him. Hanna had tried out such a student liaison once. It had been dismal. It had been, in fact, her only affair of any sort. Affairs, she now thought, were over-rated.

Breakfasting women, retired couples in pairs, and unbuffed students swarmed around her like thirsty flies, looking for a place to sit — while Hanna occupied in oblivion a table bearing only an empty cup and a yet uneaten flake of croissant. She was, of course, waiting for someone.

A girl went by on a purple Vespa, long blond hair streaming from under her purple helmet. Hanna once had wanted to be such a girl, when she was on her first grant and studying at the Vatican. She saw soon enough that it was an unreasonable thing to hope for, at odds with her talents and cultivated image. Allan, too, had hoped once to be someone else. A stage actor, she thought. He didn't talk about it. O'Neil or Beckett or someone else canonical. He felt blighted. Probably she had. But it was as unreasonable an aspiration as that she should have affairs.

The world is full of bemoaners, she thought. Let them get on with it.

A man came to rest opposite her, near the empty chair. She started, afraid he would sit down — or worse, ask to. But he didn't. There was an awkward waiting.

The unknown man surrendered, as he would — hostile silence was something Hanna had long practiced as a political tool and a self-defense strategy.

I'm Fedya Volkoff, he said.

Oh, yes?

A friend of Domenic's. Are you Hanna — sorry, Professor Floyd?

What can I do for you, Fedya? Fyodor?

Um, well, nothing. Say hello. I'm giving a poetry reading on Saturday and I'm passing out flyers. Have one. Here, please come, nice to meet you.

The poet Fedya Volkoff left his flyers at other

tables, all of them twisted up and thrown away when he had gone. Hanna folded hers and slipped it into the thin back pocket of her bag where she kept her schedule, where perhaps Allan would find it and go to hear Saturday afternoon poetry declaimed.

She took out the small red calendar, snapped off the rubber band, found the date, and made a penciled note. She'd tried using the calendar on the Mac but didn't like it, because it didn't like penciled notes. The pencil was a Cross, too slim and slippery to keep hold of, so that she was always dropping it on the floor or losing it down between the car seats. She supposed it was possible that the Mac felt about her the way she did about the pencil.

And finally resigned, she picked up her bag, checked in it for her phone, and left the café and its frantic croissants for her office. Since her morning lecture was in the same building she could mark student papers yet for an hour.

She did not. Instead, She drank some coffee markedly worse than that in the Essence café and thought about this Fedya and about Domenic and the girl with the purple Vespa and Allan

She had spent her life with Allan. Off and on, such as it was, when she was not working in some library, cathedral or mosque, visiting Buddhist and Shinto temples — there were a great many of those, all of them good for her career and her marriage. For the children, she knew, she had been Not

There, and they would of course spend a few years in therapy coming to terms with that. Following Daniel's lead, but they were none of them psycho-analytic virgins. They had failed marriages (Alicia, twice) and annoyed children (Daniel, twice) and problems with addiction — the little one, who could think of more things to get addicted to than an investment banker can think of exotic behaviors to commoditize. The blighting of lives was a two-way traffic. Did they deserve anything, these people? Specifically, did they deserve anything from her?

What exactly did that mean, to deserve? She pondered whether a paper could be got out of that which had anything new in it. Is there any belief system which does not think people ought to get what they deserve? What would their art look like? What they deserve would mean benefits and not just deserts. Justice, which they could not possibly deserve, and which is in short supply anyway. Ought. What a terrifying word.

Terrify. Like skinny cathedrals trying to touch the scrofulous cloud-wrapped gods, so terrify — the earth, terra, to make into earth, to bind to the sub-numinous world.

Taking only her keys, Hanna closed her office door and started up the dingy green hallway toward the stairs. Leaving her phone behind, always a good idea, her class roster and the students' papers, and her lecture notes. She would speak from memory, as usual. Grades could be posted, papers left in the office. There was, she thought, about enough time to visit the toilet.

9
The Paisley Violin

Karen McAdoo was having lunch with her husband at the Paisley Violin, a dark, almost baroque place at 10th and Grand. She had wanted to go to Marjon nearby on Earll for some clay and a box of test cones and had asked Bob if he wanted to come along. He did. That was unexpected. But then, since Bob had been put on leave now a month there were some other unexpected things, too. Karen wasn't going to ask questions. She got Bob into the Jeep as she imagined mothers must do when they drive their children to school. He even went into the shop and wandered up and down looking at the tools, the display of electric kilns, or whatever his eye fell on.

Karen's business took her only a few minutes. As she was backing out of the parking spot she looked at the time and remarked that there was a gallery nearby she wanted to look into, which she thought opened at ten.

Sure, Bob said. He said. Did he say that?

Karen was having a hard time getting used to his being around all the time, wandering from room to room, picking up things and looking them over as if they might have fallen off the moon. It was unsettling. He should, she thought, have been angry. She kept waiting for an explosion. She put a few of her best things out of harm's way.

In the gallery it was the same thing, though fortunately he didn't pick up any moon art. Reuben Green, the gallery owner, sometimes took ceramics, mostly tchotchkes or amusements. Nothing now of Karen's. Deformed teapots and something which looked like a rolling pin. What's this for? Bob asked, his hand dangerously close. Torah scrolls?

Karen cringed.

I doubt it, Reuben said, his equanimity undisturbed. The woman's a Lutheran. ASU graduate student, used to work for Mona Magdalena up in Scottsdale, before she went electronic. Ashley … um — Portland.

How on earth do you know she's Lutheran? Bob asked, peering impolitely at Reuben. That was his old way. Karen cringed more deeply..

She told me so.

You asked?

Why would I ask a thing like that, when I could see she had a Lutheran nose?

Bob didn't seem to get it. Karen began trying to discreetly edge him out.

It was because I asked, Reuben said, whether that thing was for Torah scrolls.

Bob smiled, as if a troublesome accounting error had been uncovered. So she said no, he said, I'm a Lutheran.

No, she said yes, it was a Torah with cookies inside.

Bob's face clouded with disappointment. He turned away to look at the painting which hung behind him. There were some masked figures floating on purple spaghetti and stars like the one's he used to get on math homework in grade school — he bent to look more closely. They were the same lick-on silver stars, which you could buy in a big bag for a dollar. There was also a naked girl riding a bicycle. Sort of a bicycle. Her hair was made out of purple spaghetti and wrapped around her like a strangler fig.

I don't like this much, Bob said. In fact, I don't like it at all.

Reuben kept his peace. Karen took Bob by the elbow.

Come on, she said. Let's have lunch.

Did you know this was here? Bob said, looking about the dark room with its old wood and the odd objects hanging from the rafters. It was narrow, with six tables on one long wall opposite the length of the bar. The other end led out to a dusty vacant lot. Close to where they sat was a piano.

So where's the violin?

Over there. Karen pointed toward the door. In the case.

Bob twitched as if he were going to get up, but then beached his skepticism and subsided. Karen tugged on her lower lip. Yet another new thing.

It was while they were eating their stew that

two old men came in, one with a sheaf of papers and the other with a guitar case. Behind the piano the guitar player found a music stand. He divvied up the sheet music with the piano player.

After some plinking and bonging the two began to play some quiet jazz, introspective riffs handed back and forth, some call and response passages, a summary statement from the piano — the sort of music heard in smoky bars and clubs on foggy nights sixty years before.

Bob was entranced. He forgot to eat. The set finished, the guitarist went out to smoke, and the pianist ambled over to their table and sat unceremoniously down.

You seemed to like the music, he said. He had an old voice, quiet, a bit whispery, comfortable like his piano.

Very much, Karen said, actually meaning it. Do you play here often?

Every couple of weeks. For fun, as much as anything. Ed and I have worked together for years. I guess we must know each other about perfectly. In the music. We used to work places up and down the coast. Too old for that, when just get together now and then and jam.

The pianist talked for a while, not saying much but only talking pleasantly, until Ed returned and the two of them went up to play another set. Ed smiled at Karen and Bob, just a twinkle and a faint lift of a corner of his mouth. He met the pianist's eye briefly, arpeggiated a chord, and they were off on a winding tune which Bob was sure he recognized.

Karen went over to the bar and brought back two more beers. They sat on, listening, until finally it was over and the two friends gathered up their music and put away the guitar and the music stand and shook hands. Karen gave Ed ten dollars.

I hope we'll hear you again, she said.

Well, said the piano player, we don't play regular dates. There's places where we just drop in, more or less.

Maybe here, then.

No. This place closes next month.

Bob, who had levered himself onto his feet, overheard this and sat down again. His stomach turned.

Round midnight, Bob said on the way home. Round midnight. Thelonius Monk. That's what it was.

What do you know about jazz? Karen said, surprised again.

Did you know about that place? he asked two blocks later.

I've been there. They never had music.

Lunch, Bob proposed.

A beer. You were at some conference.

Well, you won't go again, apparently.

So you're done with that, Bob said. It's all done with, he said as Karen turned the Jeep into their driveway. She switched off the engine but didn't unfasten her seat belt.

Bob, Karen said, catching his meaning, that's over. That was done with already.

Oh, was it? Well, it's over now, anyway.

Yes, she said, with a note of unplaceable regret.

I could get three months from H&R Block, I suppose.

They're not going to take you back, are they?

No. I'm fifty-nine. There will be social security, a pension, some small investments… Why should they? We'll live small.

We already live small.

Do we? Yes, I suppose we do.

You haven't said why, Karen observed after a long silence. It's been a month and you haven't said anything about why they put you on leave.

No, Bob said, and said nothing else.

Bob, she said. You're a jerk.

Am I?

He, too, had not released his seat belt. He shifted restlessly under it.

You're a bitch, yourself, he said at last.

There was a bird sitting on a low branch of the old olive growing beside the driveway. A mockingbird. Having seen enough, it flew away.

That tree must be as old as my grandfather, Bob said.

Your grandfather's dead.

As old as he would be, then. Why did you marry me if I was a jerk?

You weren't a jerk then. You got to be one.

Did I?

Yes.

You didn't get to be a bitch. Bob observed. You just were one.

Oh. Well, then, you see?

I notice, Bob said, that woman next door started pulling down her shades.

She got a boyfriend, I think, Karen said.

The two of them continued to sit for a while in silence. Then Karen stirred, and both unclipped their belts together.

We ought to go somewhere, Bob said as they walked slowly side by side across the grass to the front door. Just anywhere.

There's a train to Seattle, Karen said. We could take the train.

I'd like that, Bob said. I haven't been to Seattle in years. That was for a conference or something, I suppose. You get the top bunk, though.

You jerk, Bob, Karen said. She unlocked the front door.

II

LANDFALL

McAdoo Moored

Bob McAdoo, now that he had been downsized — or laid off, he couldn't decide which — was spending a lot of his time home alone. He had no reason to go out so he didn't. He didn't want to go out. The world was full of obnoxious people and he might find himself talking to one. Karen was either in the studio where she didn't like to be bothered, and anyway she always had the radio on if she were glazing or trimming — disasters and politicians and injustices — or if she were throwing, some repetitive rhythmic music which made Bob's legs crawl. Bolero. Philip Glass — or else she was out somewhere. Networking, he supposed. Intended to suppose. Women were always supposed to be always networking. In reality she was probably screwing someone.

Bob's mentality was inclined to purdah, a discreet form of the more confrontational burka. Discreet purdah was a good practice for an accountant whose business was to conceal the truth. Not necessarily falsify it, but like a priest or anyone at the top of some hieratic system of knowledge, the literate in a world of illiterates, to control those who know not. Had he desired to be the shaman or bard in his nest, sought out for oracles. Concealment was not, however, a useful strategy for an accountant suspected of irregularities inconveniently concealed from those who would have to explain them to boards, committees, and clients. Of course, anyone can be conveniently suspected of anything convenient to suspect. So Bob had been discreetly disposed of, out the back door of the casbah, for the very thing he was good at: lying. Really they were just inconvenient mistakes.

The pencil-bouncer was behind it, of course. It was to do ultimately with the water glass incident. Everything is connected eventually, be it stories on the night the last one is told, or the planets with the sun when it becomes a red giant.

Aside from the salary, however, he had never much liked the work. It required too much concentration. It was too meticulous. Aside from the money, Bob preferred his present way of life, now that some time had passed and he had learned that nothing would be expected of him. That he was not at risk of being pointed out or jeered at.

At first he read books, then newspapers. He took walks, very early when no one was about. After a while it was computer solitaire and crossword puzzles. Then nothing. He got up late. He stopped shaving regularly. He stopped getting dressed. He took showers and forgot to put anything on at all. Karen sewed the drapes together. Finally roused by this from his snake-like torpor, by a spring-time need for warmth and sunlight, Bob put on some underwear, a nearly new red pinstripe shirt, and a blue suit. Knotting his tie, he went out and returned with a bookkeeper's job for a string of espresso franchises.

He had no interest in actual coffee shops, or for that matter coffee. He drank it, but didn't care where it came from. But then he began to have trouble balancing his books. He went out to observe, for him an unprecedented curiosity about evidence, an unheard of attempt to map his columns of numbers onto the world of chairs and tables, raspberry bars under glass, used paper cups, baristas, and janitors at 3 am.

He traced the problem to a particular store. Receipts were going into employees' pockets. This meant that coffee, pastries, cups, and employee hours had to reappear, to be resurrected from the grave of the eaten, the discarded, the wasted, in order to balance the disappearing receipts. The discrepancy had arisen like Lazarus because too many people had their hands in the till, because nobody knew for sure what a kilo of roasted beans or a thousand plastic coffee cup lids or ten pounds of fruit bars actually cost, or even for sure what their own salaries were before taxes and benefits and subventions and other whatnot. Bob, who after all was not very bright, was still illuminated enough to catch these beclouded thieves.

Now what? Constitutionally unwilling to risk a simple unqualified statement about anything. including the statement of an account, constitutionally unable to ask the employees for an account of themselves, Bob did nothing, the same unrealpolitik which had done him in before.

Nothing wasn't going to work this time,

though. Bob erased coffee, napkins, milk, bagels as fast as he could, but covering up for these idiots was like boxing with a windmiller. Finally he had to admit defeat. The whole scheme was exposed. There were angry people everywhere. To his surprise, Bob received a commendation and a small bonus for initiative which he used for beer and chips, annoying Karen who liked neither.

Bob, she said, leaving the rest unsaid. As unexplained as a discrepancy in the books. Bob remembered how his mother had stayed at the office past midnight, hand-cranking the calculator in search of an errant nine. It was a detective story, only it turned out that the two did it.

Bob allowed himself an enigmatic Buddha's smile.

Mudras they're called, he said. These smiles. I googled them.

Bob, you idiot. It's to do with the hands, not the face.

Bob's smile grew by the tiniest amount.

The Last Of Dugan

Dugan's self-writing autobiography was serializing itself on his blog. Every morning Dugan got out of bed to see what he'd said about himself during the night. He wasn't used to being awake in the morning. Perhaps he wasn't. Awake. He wasn't used to being a character in a novel, either. The thing was, he was finding both of these things interesting and was loath to go back to the old way. It was just that his grades were suffering. Perhaps he ought to change out his classes for something more appropriate — a seminar on Barthes or quantum physics. Reading his autobiography — really it wasn't auto, more like panto — might prove to be transformational. That was a long step beyond merely interesting.

This had been going on for several weeks now. His life had almost caught up with itself, and in another week Dugan would begin to see how things would turn out. Whatever was going on, he was too curious to stop it. He was also a little afraid of interrupting his self-writing autobiography for fear of interrupting something else. He could just have stopped reading it, which was a little like a child thinking his mother would go away if he closed his eyes, or if God stopped paying attention. Other people would continue to read about him. Dugan's RSS feeds had gone way up since his life began, as well as the number of independent IPs, first time visitors, and other measures of interest. His measly little blog had gone from about 2000 visitors a month to five times that simply by word of mouth, Facebook shares, and retweets. He was being read all over the world.

Dugan briefly entertained the idea of figuring out what was going on in order to market the thing as a ghost-writing app but gave such tinkering up as probably dangerous.

According to his autobiographer, Dugan had

grown up in a midwestern village of 900 people with one store and a grain elevator. Except for the owner of the store, everyone's income was dependent on the price of wheat, corn, and soybeans. Some farmers raised cattle and pigs but it was hard to make this pay. About half the adults in town tithed, the rest paid what they could, and the town rubbed along, dying more slowly than most, likely to be buried about 2005 at the age of 120. And this had proved to be true. Dugan himself had been gone twenty-five years when that happened, and he didn't bother to go to the funeral.

All this was approximately true of the embodied Dugan. The autobiographical one was ten years old than he was, and the town of Dugan was only about half the size of the one he actually did grow up in. This sort of thing was on public record. It wouldn't have been hard for his autobiographer to look up the known facts about Dugan and invent something similar. Where the facts were lacking, the writer's imagination was proving to be astute. The cases of child molestation, for example, were pretty much as Dugan knew them to have been, and the molesters themselves were about right — the coach of the eight-man football team, the farmer whose wife had died of cancer who took to molesting his youngest daughter, the grocer who let certain people run a tab in exchange for silence on matters which were not their business anyway. Dugan's autobiographer also guessed the suicide of a middle-aged bachelor living about ten miles north of town on sixty acres, half of which was a slough most years. Some people thought he had simply starved to death, but most knew better.

There being no bar or liquor store, and the teetotaling grocer refusing to stock beer, everyone went to a larger town in the neighboring state to buy beer and whiskey. No one drank wine in those days. Bourbon and scotch were drunk by the better-off. The poor and the teenagers drank Budweiser, even on holidays. After school — a consolidated school in the next town, a hundred students in all grades — the teens who had cars drove out to the river with a six-pack and made out. Some of the younger ones rode along if they were in favor, but they didn't get any of the beer.

It seemed that Dugan's autobiographer knew quite a lot about life in such places, but personal experience of that sort was not hard to get. Such towns abound between the Rockies and the Mississippi, from Canada down into Texas. It was when his autobiographer began to delve into Dugan's inner life that there was some divergence. It turned out, for example, that Dugan hated his mother, who was a controlling woman; nothing ever came out of her mouth but advice. She was also a hypocritical moralist — simultaneous with her preaching she conducted a long affair with her brother-in-law, a fat drunk who beat his own wife. Dugan's own father, it developed, was a skinny man who was a moderate drinker and beat his children instead. He had been disappointed in life and took this means of mollifying himself.

At this point in the story readers began to comment. What was wrong with Dugan's father, it came out in reply to questioning, was one short leg. It had been injured in a power takeoff accident as a boy and had made him the butt of jokes all through school. He was also impotent much of the time, which accounted for some other troubles, and the grain dust had ruined his lungs. He could just about read and write. The woman he'd married had been pretty enough down by the river but after six children had become misshapen and ugly. There were some other more sordid items on the list.

To Dugan his autobiographical father was a bit over-determined. But in fact he had not liked either of his parents for roughly these reasons. From the time he was ten it was obvious that he could not live in this town, but his parents had caused him to move out ahead of sequence, leaving behind two older sisters. Probably they got molested afterwards. Dugan had never been sure about that. The one time he saw them, at his mother's funeral, he hadn't asked. Dugan's autobiographical father had died of blood poisoning after taking some buckshot in the shoulder from his brother-in-law's pheasant gun. His actual father had died of natural causes, to Dugan's present annoyance. In some respects his autobiography was proving to be better than his everyday life.

When Dugan's autobiographer made the quantum leap into the future, these comparisons of course came to an end, and Dugan's interest became simple and unsophisticated. All he wanted to know was how it was going to end.

The Coffee Lab again, where it all began when Dugan impulsively walked off with that flash drive. He had wanted to sneak a peek. Someone was running around naked with the drapes open. But — a mirror looks back; a laser pointer points both ways; everything has a return address; dark matter connects us all, filling up what was once empty space to make a suffocating plenum.

Four tables away, at the back of the room, a woman with long blond hair was arguing with a half-dozen men. All of them had identical books lying on the table, held down by one spread, protective hand. The woman poked the table with her index finger as if she were chasing a spider. Several others broke in loudly. Again and again loudly. They were all loud. It wasn't hard to understand that they were a Bible study group which had been hijacked by this woman into an argument on transcendentalism.

Odd. Dugan moved up a table, then another, listening with professional ears. The woman knew what she was talking about; the men were all clueless. The Protestant rejection of transubstantiation, the triune God, the ineffability of numbers, Plato's numinous Forms, a priori knowledge, Taoism — the woman talked over every flurry of irrelevant chapter and verse. The direction of her attack was toward the materialist salient of conservative belief. Resurrection of the Spirit in bodily form. Spirits. Do spirits have arms and legs? Twats? Are they immortal? So why would they want to be trapped in a body again? Not immortal. If they breed, maybe they do have twats. Making little spirits. The Trump trumps, but they've gone extinct while they were waiting.

Chorus of outrage.

Entering into, she said contemptuously. What is there to enter into after a billion years? After the sun goes nova?

Nova? One of the men snorted. At last here was something he knew about. The sun isn't big enough to go nova, he said. When its hydrogen is gone it will become a red giant. The earth will lose mass and move out to a wider orbit, but it will be burnt up anyway.

Is this before or after the Trump? We're talking Apocalypse here. Revelations sixteen one pour out the vials of the wrath of God upon the earth.

That sent everyone scrambling, the mystical book of visions not having heretofore excited much interest. But it should have, for the woman now let out an invective of citations. The spirit entering into and the resurrection of bodies whose atoms had long been absorbed into rocks —

Wrath, she said. Cool word. And the mome wraths outgrabe.

This put an end to the discussion. Books slammed shut. Bodies rose up. The blond woman slipped away.

Dugan was waiting outside when she emerged.

Who are you? she challenged when he approached.

My name's Dugan. I couldn't help hearing —

Dugan, she said, breaking into a smile. She had a wonderful wide mouth. Dugan. You're the one who's been blogging about your mother's getting blind drunk with the high school quarterback and —

Well, no, that's — it's complicated. Why were you arguing with those guys? There didn't seem to be any point. You're not going to convince —

No point.

Now look, Dugan said. You got some things wrong.

Of course. Whatever they say, you speak against it. It's what they do, so why —

Who are you, then?

Ashley Portland, she said, smiling even more broadly and holding out her hand. It was hard and dry. She put on a motorcycle helmet which had been strapped to her bag, dumped the bag into the seat compartment of a scooter parked one slot over, and got on. Let's go, she said.

Dugan slid onto the seat behind her. One kick brought to scooter to snarly tenor life and the two of them squirted out onto Farmer and away south into the Mitchell neighborhood of traffic circles and little pre-war houses behind hedges of prickly pear or covered in vines like hair and old Datsuns parked in the driveways.

This fortuitous meeting convinced Dugan to kill his blog.

But it didn't like that. A few days later it started up again on its own and began a campaign of self-hatred and sordid revelations about his soon-ended relationship with Ashley. Readership jumped into five figures. His new blog persona began to talk about killing first himself, then other people. After he described an evisceration in unpleasant detail Ashley called the police. Social services or suicide watch or somebody came and took him away.

Satisfied, the blog went silent.

Sister

Dido Makros was by preference a solitary animal. Not a hermit, though he could easily have become one, but merely a person who did not wish to be in the company of others.

Dido lived in a burrow-like house dug into the side of Camelback Mountain. When he did go out, to sit in Encanto Park to watch the joggers, dog walkers, picnickers, and other old people like himself sitting on benches watching joggers, dog walkers, and picnickers, he was aware that this pleasure was a little thin but he could not think of others. He went to coffee shops and sat in libraries. In the Phoenix public library, in the main branch which straddled the hurrying I-10 tunnel, there was a small gallery off the entrance which he liked to visit, and one day he noticed there a brochure for First Fridays. A bus tour of artists' studios, the brochure said, would began at the library at 6pm, and on Roosevelt Row a few blocks away many of the galleries would be open. A studio visit would probably be too claustrophobic, although the bus ride was attractive. Dido pondered this, rubbed his cheek, and set off on foot. And so it happened that on the first Friday in January a man who thought three people was a crowd was strolling among the winter visitors, people in town for the Fiesta Bowl, scruffy locals, families with double-wide prams, and anonymous people with inscrutable intentions at Roosevelt and Second Street.

He looked into Carly's Bistro but there was no place to sit. Farther up, one side of the street was occupied by artists' apartments over a string of small shops, most of which were either unoccupied or given over to shawls and buttons and hair salons, some identified on the tour guide as being galleries. One or two framed somethings. A storefront gallery on the other side of the street looked promising. He crossed over, but hesitated. Two other people were there, talking with a third, probably the gallery minder, who was a young man sitting on a folding stool at the rear of the single room.

Nevertheless, he went in.

A dozen paintings were on offer, ten of them

by one artist, with no stock or reserve, as if it all would be packed into the back of a van at the end of the evening, leaving the former gallery windows still bleared and unwashed, waiting for the next First Friday. Dido's inspection of the perfunctory paintings quickly became a pretense. Instead, he gave an ear to what the three people at the back were saying.

The minder was an ASU student. One of the others was certainly the artist, but whether of the ten or the two Dido could not guess. The third was a man in his thirties, well-dressed but without a tie and altogether somewhat rumpled. He stood with his hands in his pockets, one foot deferentially hooked behind the other as if about to polish the toe of his shoe on his pants. Despite appearances, this was clearly a person of authority. And suddenly he turned to Dido, pointing electrically.

You! he said. What do you think of this?

Dido bridled. A person wearing a red foulard and carrying a two-hundred-year-old sword stick ought not, he thought, be addressed as You.

On the floor, leaning against the minder's stool, was a small unframed painting which Dido had not noticed. The man picked it up, holding it negligently by one stretcher, and beckoned Dido forward.

Oh, Dido began, uncertain. There was something both harried and hopeful in the painter's face, and when his eyes fell expectantly on Dido there was no possibility of remaining silent. So

Dido took a careful breath and embarked on his analysis. Color; composition — Dido pointed out an atavistic desire for a centripetal organization based on the golden mean —

A spiral, the well-dress man said.

Yes.   Resulting   in   the   disorganized brushstrokes here, and here — Dido pointed with his stick — they dissipate the energy, don't you think —

Dido broke off, unnerved by the abashed young painter and by the intensity of the well-dressed man's gaze.

So, said the gallery minder. Maybe we can find some wall space for this next to your other two?

The painter skittered out. A middle-aged couple came in. The minder stood up. The well-dressed man put out his hand to Dido

Gordon Brisbane, he said. Representing Magdalena Gallery.

Sisters, it was, said Dido, pleased to have a safe reply. Was called Sisters at one time. I've been in.

Some time ago. We're digital now.

This put an end to the obvious strategies and Dido, not knowing what to do next, did nothing. He took back his hand. Gordon returned his to his pocket. There was an exchange of smiles, one broad and one faint.

Come across with me to Carly's, Gordon Brisbane said. There's bound to be a place at the bar by now. We can talk. Dido assented, Gordon took him discreetly by the elbow, steering him across the intersection, into the bistro, to the two seats predicted. Gordon nattered all the while in a quiet voice which nevertheless somehow managed to be heard through the din. And so Dido was obliged to introduce himself, more loudly than Gordon, to this oppressively persuasive man of a sort never to be found on a bench in Encanto Park, overheard he was sure by those people who were now jogging his elbow, pressing familiarly against his back, and breathing on his cheek.

Gordon held out a business card. Dido took it, held it by the edges between thumb and forefinger.

Come out to Mona's sometime and have a look. Quieter, too.

He looked sharply at the woman breathing on Dido's neck, who looked sharply away. Gordon melted into the crowd. Dido put his glass of beer, still full, on the counter and pushed his way back out onto the street where a woman with a chirrupy voice accosted him from behind.

Excuse me, you forgot this.

That was the tip, Dido said, nettled by her phenomenally lame excuse. She was wearing a chirrupy-colored shirt and an elaborate tattoo which ran right across between her shoulders and deep down out of sight between her breasts.

I couldn't help hearing, she began unwisely

—

Yes, you could help, Dido snapped. He had

not spoken that way to anyone since his mother.

that —

Dido turned on his heel.

Excuse me —

Astounded by the woman's blithe persistence, Dido confronted her. The tattoo, at first just a design, proved to be a hieratic eagle with outspread wings, head in profile, and probably somewhere unseen a fasces in its talons. She had shoulder-length blond hair and carried a purple motorcycle helmet. I used to work for Mona, she said, putting out a damp hand.

Ah. So you know this Brisbane fellow.

Yes, she said, cutting off anything more.

And what are you now? Dido asked, taking the other option.

A potter. Come and see my stuff. She handed him yet another card, put on her purple helmet and, message delivered, bobbed away up the street. The crowd was beginning to thin. Dido turned in the opposite direction, back toward Central Avenue, looking thoughtfully at the two cards.

What had happened was the sort of thing which always made him very anxious. He felt accounted for. Known. Fitted into some transcendental scheme like the criminal in a detective story who must be found out, without whom there is no story.

Ashley was her name, and her card lay on the half-round table in his foyer for several weeks. Finally he made up his mind and drove across town to see for himself. The work was interesting. He returned a week later. And so, inevitably, because he was in the grip of a world in which there are no loose ends, he met Karen McAdoo.

Karen was fascinated by this little man, dapper as woodpecker, careful as a chipmunk. With some difficulty she persuaded him to meet her on Friday at Cibo on Fifth Avenue and Fillmore. This was on Thursday. Two days' time was too much. The chipmunk's nerve failed and he stood her up. Karen ate her wood-fired artichoke pizza alone, outdoors on the plaza under the sparkling electric candles, watching the traffic on the Avenue and chatting with two men at the next table. She took a box for the half of the pizza intended for Dido, skipped the nine dollar crêpe fresca, ordered a double espresso, and changed seats.

A mistake. One of them was an accountant, the other a county bureaucrat. The possibility they would know Bob was high. That put any flirting beyond the pale, and Karen was briefly angry with Bob for interfering. She neglected, out of caution, to ask their names.

Meeting someone, she said apologetically, indicating the doggie box. She judged these were the sort of men who would need a reason for a woman to be eating alone. Last minute affairs.

Slowly the easy banter which had earlier prevailed returned. A round of microbrews. The bureaucrat was a beer connoisseur who knew all about this beer, seemingly down to the name of the rat which had drowned in the tank. Karen went easy. The crêpe fresca returned, shared among the three of them. More beer. Consideration given to bruschetta or something of the sort. The meal was going backwards.

The possibilities remained, however, unconsummated. Despite Bob's perennial fears, Karen had never had a one-night stand, or anything more serious. She sometimes regretted that, wondered whether it were a character flaw, tried it out as a thought experiment. The satisfaction was momentary. She dressed quietly and went out to the studio.

There was some not unpleasant fiddling with knees and fingers with the bureaucrat. Karen excused herself to go and look for her errant dinner companion. It was too complicated to settle the bill, so she put down cash for the tip.

It didn't take long to locate a man like Dido Makros, who fancied himself to be secretive but was completely naive about secrets. He even had a doorbell. On Sunday morning she showed up on Dido's doorstep with the styrofoam pizza box. Dido, victimized by the same reluctant politeness which had made him accept Ashley Portland's gallery invitation in the first place, invited her to come in. He took the pizza and excused himself to put it away. Karen waited in the foyer, noticing the things on the table: the Sunday newspaper, a magazine (*Art News*), an unopened letter addressed to

Gospodin Fyodor Fyodorovitch Makros (post-marked two weeks earlier), and on top of the pile, a black leather hat belonging to The Man With No Name. She replaced these things as she found them. The foyer was bare of other furniture. The terrazzo floor was made with an embedded design, vaguely Hopi, and the walls were of what were probably local chunks of granite. A soft enclosing sunshine filled it, brought in through the mountain-side through light tubes. Dido returned empty-handed, soft-footed in leather moccasins. Karen took off her hiking boots and followed in her socks.

There was a morning room — of sorts. The windowless house unnerved her. A service of tea stood on a low table. A teapot, a thermos of hot water, two tea bowls, small dishes of sugar and tea with silver spoons, a tiny cream pitcher. Dido filled the pot, waited for ninety seconds in silence while it brewed, and then poured.

Perhaps you know these bowls, he said shyly. Japanese, 17th century.

Karen looked at her slightly mis-shaped tea bowl more carefully, turned it, lifted it up to look at the bottom. She drank the tea.

No, she said. Are they famous?

Dido laughed, just a murmur and two breaths. Not famous, he admitted. I meant rather as a style of pottery.

Well, yes. Yes, as that.

This exhausted possible topics of small talk.

The situation was peculiar. Indirectly, since the original invitation had been hers, Karen was the hostess in her host's house. He, the coerced guest, was comfortable with indefinite silence, whereas she became fidgety and unhappy. She had prepared to flee when this seemingly ever-courteous little Greek-Russian gentleman rescued her.

I have very few guests here, he said. You are in fact the first this year. A welcome novelty. Thank you for your persistence.

You live alone?

Yes, yes — alone. I would find it difficult to endure. I go out when the maid comes. The rest of the housework I do myself.

Maids, she said.

Yes. A service.

Well if you go out, Karen began brashly —

Dido saw her intent at once and explained about the park.

So then, um — Karen did not feel safe with any form of address — I don't know what to call you.

Dido, he said. In my case, this is the diminutive of Theodore. My parents anglicized the name before I was baptized. Gospodin as you undoubtedly know is a formal mode of address quite inappropriate for this humble person, which is why I've left the envelope unopened.

Creepy. Too noticing a person.

Your husband is, I believe, Robert McAdoo? I

have some knowledge of that unfortunate accident in the Magdalena gallery.

Oh. You were there?

No. I'm not a collector, you see, and a gallery opening would be would be a quite futile nuisance — Dido left it open how he came to know about Bob's downfall. Where can one see your work? He went on.

I have a gallery in Tucson, Karen said, feeling inexplicably diffident. He seemed to know what she was going to say before she did. Consignments here and there, she admitted. Gift shops for tourists, 5th Avenue in Scottsdale, the airport, there's a little museum there you know.

I didn't.

Local fairs, word of mouth, open studio — it's a scramble. I tried the art fair circuit once. Too grueling.

Despite his unsettling knowingness and his nearly suppressed phobias, Dido's kindly and elaborate way of speaking was as reassuring as the mattress in a children's play room. Karen became a little giddy. Then, just as had happened in the restaurant the night before, she seemed to trip on something in the grass. Fatally self-conscious, she cringed to realize how she was dressed, almost in studio clothes. She felt as coy and false as she must have seemed to those two men, unable to carry through her plan. Dumb with embarrassment, wanted to flee.

Dido was studying Karen with a speculative

expression. She had suddenly gone silent, as if her plug had come loose, then just as suddenly sprang to life, sprang to her feet, made some excuses, and backed hastily out of the room. In the foyer she soon abandoned an attempt to put her hiking boots back on and escaped with them in her hand.

From the open doorway he watched her go. His hand lay on the bronze lever. His smile was small. Someone as awkward as himself, he thought.

Not far down the street was a place where the mountainside fell away steeply and a low wall had been built along the edge of the road. Karen sat down on the wall to put on her shoes. From this perch she could see across to the Estrella Mountains which bounded the southern edge of the valley. Traffic was light on a Sunday morning. The dry air was decently clear, but not so clear as it once was. In January, at this hour of the morning, the shadowed air was cold, but where the sun struck it made her skin feel as it did when she'd been slapped. Dido's house was on the south side of the mountain and the low winter sun on this wall caught her full. She walked on a short distance to a pullout where she'd parked her old car.

An old car as unpresentable as its driver. What had come over her? First the restaurant, now this. It was something to do with Bob, with Bob's new-found self-sufficiency. Her doings no longer mattered to him. She was on her own. She was re-

tired from her old self. She was free to be as cyni-
cal and bitchy as she wanted to be. The thing was,
she needed practice. In Bob's time she had been
playing a part. Here was a chance for the real
thing.

She had never wanted to be anyone's sister,
big or little. Big or little, sisterhood made her feel
like things ought to add up, that they would add
up. So long as everyone stood in their place the
sisterhood would hold together like a balance
sheet, a part of the greater good. That was Bob's
view, though he was least like a brother than anyone she knew. Bob would never be seen at Cibo
with another guy after work, putting down marga-
ritas and bruschettas and hustling the single woman at the next table. Casually amused, because they
were with each other. Women who are together
with each other only until they can re-pair are not
sisters. What Karen meant was that she was not
family

Now that Bob had discovered himself as the
minus two on the balance sheet which held the
world together he was at peace.

From the mountain, Karen looked out on this
strip of city which flowed through what appeared
to be a gap but was really a small sea which did
not flow but clawed tidally at the enclosing land,
out of which this mountain rose like an isolated
rock, a threat to ships making for harbor. Her
house — what used to be hers and Bob's house —
was down there in the shallow water.

Bob's world was the accounting world of plate techtonics in which all the land is one mass connected at the root on which the sea lay like puddles after a rainstorm. Bob's was the world of brothers and sisters.

Karen's was the seafaring world in which rocks and mountains and continents are flotsam in the surf, soon worn away and forgotten. Once or twice she had stood on the shore and gazed at this mirror world and then turned again inland, back to the business of turning mud into rock. It was Bob's business to be increasing the orderliness of things. But that was Bob's business.

She turned to look out of the back window back towards Dido's house, the Gospodin burrow hidden just beyond the curve, speculating on which sort of man he was.

She started the car and drove a way, down the mountain, the engine coughing a little, down the switchbacks which were the rivulets flowing off the piled-up rubble to the beach.

The Tycoon

Now a widower, under circumstances which he hoped were mysterious to everyone, Allan Floyd sold his house in Paradise Valley and bought a condo downtown on a mid-level floor of a tower near the Heard Museum. He took a big loss on the house. The owner of the condo took a big loss. It came out even.

Other than in the summer — it was now July — it was would be just possible for Allan to walk anywhere, a considerable novelty. Pedestrians were odd at any time of year, of course, except farther south near the University's Downtown Campus. Students are expected to walk.

While summer loomed Allan began to think what he could do about it. He mentioned this to another of the residents on his floor, a man with whom he had already exchanged a few remarks in the elevator and was thus approachable. Allan had thought he was making small talk about the weather and was alarmed to be taken seriously. This man, it seemed, owned a timeshare which he was anxious to dispose of. In a few moments Allan had, like some hero who climbs Mt McKinley in patent leather shoes, become the owner of a month's worth of apartment somewhere in southern California.

Tentative owner. Sublettor. Lessee. Part of a building. In Encinitas. The man's name was Martin. Martin Something. Allan was invited for a drink to settle the arrangement.

Martin believed, he said, that Allan lived alone, and Martin believed that he did.

A companion, perhaps? Was welcome.

No. Regrettably dead. Presumably. A curious expression rose into Martin's face. Dead, Allan added hastily. Not presumably regrettable. Regretted.

Martin kept a companion, apparently a companion, to whom Allan was introduced. Marta Something. Martin's condo was exactly like Allan's except for the companion and the pictures on the walls. Allan owned no pictures nor anything else which might be hung on a wall. Marta gave him a glass of red wine. She herself was drinking coffee.

After a time some brie appeared. Allan was asked whether in addition to leasing the time share he would pay a premium for the summer privilege. But this, along with the art and the companion and the twenty stories, was one condition too many for Allan. The deal fell through.

Nevertheless, there was a change in Allan's life because of Martin's near miss. The companion, too often alone, invited him back for another glass of wine and by August, when he was to have been in Encinitas, Allan had acquired the companion instead. Taken a sub-lease on. Proof of concept was the term in Allan's business. She did not ask about his ex-wife (deceased) and soon he and Marta were getting along quite well.

But Marta was not, he saw, a woman to take inconvenient risks, and she did eventually want to know more about her predecessor. Hanna, said her relict, had been an art historian.

Marta pondered this, and after giving him a second glass of wine she asked whether Allan knew much about art.

Not a scrap, he said.

Nor did she, Marta replied.

Together they toured the rooms. There were pictures everywhere, even in the bathroom and the bedrooms. She and Martin had separate bedrooms, and Marta was of the opinion that hers had been given the inferior pictures. .

Did she like any of them?

Marta made an eloquent gesture of indifference. Martin had taken her to museums and galleries, she had been introduced everywhere, but made nothing of it. The coffee prevented her from falling asleep and she went home early.

Allan pressed her for details of this society to which she had entrée. He was interested in few things so much as entrée. Marta named collectors and gallery owners. Allan made visits. He made no pretense of knowledge in anything other than investment opportunity. One gallery intrigued him — it had no shop, no address, no means for someone like Allan, dependent on innuendo, implication, and veiled expression, to do business. All it had was a slide show and an e-mail address.

Marta said she would make arrangements. These were mysteriously made and one afternoon Allan and his entrée drove up to Cave Creek to see Mona Magdalena..

They were admitted by someone named Gordon, who offered them a viewing. But Gordon had the alertness of someone used to negotiating with prickly, defensive artists and quickly sensed Allan's resistance to any such waste of time. When a few discreet questions discovered that this was an art collector with no liking for art, Gordon vanished. After some time, which Allan spent looking at incomprehensible scribbles, Mona appeared, winkled out of some far refuge, persuaded to return to the flesh.

Marta had in fact been sitting unnoticed all this while in collected stillness. Now she stood up in one fluid motion, like a dancer or a yogin, and took charge of the conversation.

Both Mona and Allan soon knew how the matter stood between them, and Marta's interventions, as the — possibly former — representative of a genuine collector, helped to cover any accidental crassness. Allan was invited to return.

However, it soon became clear that Allan as usual had over-estimated his own importance. It was Marta who closed the deal, and within two months she had abandoned Allan and Martin both, along with the condo and Martin's leftover privileges.

Allan barely noticed. He liked Mona. He liked Gordon, whose amused disdain was apparently general and not meant for him. There was a woman with an Austrian double eagle tattooed on her breasts who showed up now and then on a motorcycle. He liked her, too. She never stayed long and left Gordon in a foul mood. He was giving her money. Allan saw her tuck a check into the leather messenger bag she always carried on a long strap over her shoulder, to which her helmet was clipped. Allan declined to ask Gordon about this. He didn't want his own finances audited, either.

In September he moved out from his condo to Mona's house. He borrowed a small room there. He kept small and quiet, drank his afternoon goblet of red wine slowly in a corner of the sunny, open reception area, furnished and painted in Mexican décor, where he contemplated the irregularities of the wood plank floor, barely aware of conversations elsewhere in the house.

He had not used to like conversations which he could not overhear. He had considered them stealthy and had felt aggrieved.

Allan was now fully engaged with some other men in an enterprise which easily provided him the means for a modest lifestyle — now modest, with the demise of the immodest Hanna. Some of the excess he invested in the gallery. He supposed it could be said that he was laundering this money, but for tax purposes it simply went away and never came back, having never been there in the first place. Allan thought of it as more or less an anonymous charity and thought no more. "Recognized" was a technical term to which he had been introduced early on when he couldn't get his network printer to work. Fedya said it was because the computer didn't recognize it, rather as if the poor printer were too vulgar for the society in which it found itself. After that Allan used the word often. It was a form of snobbery. Allan didn't mind admitting that he was a snob. That had been one of the sources of friction between him and Hanna, because Hanna had been the superior snob.

Six months after his wife's disappearance Allan sat down with Mona and drew up a formal contract. When he stood up again, after two glasses of wine, he was part owner of an art gallery. What he had agreed to was that, in return for paying the gallery's operating expenses, he would receive a percentage of sales. The percentage was small, trivial in fact. It was intended as earnest money for other arrangements to come. Allan, pleased with his new status as Maecenas, was pleased to ask no questions about arrangements. He had never been much of a man to consider the future, except with respect to games like chess which he had never played but took to be an enterprise like that on which he was presently engaged.

So it was that a ménage came into being as intriguing to Allan it might have been to a boy in a new treehouse. Gordon was left to the artists, Mona was left to the collectors, Marta provided the lubricant, and nothing was expected of Allan at all. This was most agreeable. His business could be kept conveniently obscure as the people with whom he now lived cared nothing about it and in other respects he was, in a way, hiding out. Everything was worked through proxies including, he was assured, the communications, data mining, transactions and correspondence necessary to his business. Officially he lived in a mid-town condominium near the museum. Difficult or, he hoped, impossible to locate, he could go about things without interference. He sold the Mercedes and, since he no longer had a car, either he was picked up by taxi or Marta drove him.

He was enjoying the role of éminence grise. If there were to be any artists Gordon went along but, smooth as ink as he was, Gordon preferred the company of those artists who were raw and up-coming and needed a marinade. Marta, who had found out she was comfortable with everyone, could put a squirrel at ease. And so the gallery's influence grew, and the gallery's sales grew, and Allan's return on investment grew — slightly — and Gordon's upcomers became more willing to polish off the crotchets and rugosities from their art, and the art went along on its own, disregarded, powered by some energy which was a welcome mystery.

And so did Allan. In March of 2012, eleven months after Hanna's mortal disappearance, Allan Floyd was taken away and never heard from again.

Spring is the season for arrests, Gordon re-marked dryly, and nobody suggested it might have been anything else. That summer the gallery made a large sale and there was some discussion as to whether Allan was owed anything. Gordon sug-gested an escrow but Mona laughed this off. She had never liked Allan and was not about to like him now, even though her operating expenses con-tinued to be paid by some mechanism she was loath to investigate. Marta thought this was a bit crass.

When Marta went back to Martin's condo to retrieve some jewelry which Martin had appropriated, the concierge told her in confidence that her neighbor, erstwhile neighbor Allan Floyd, had mysteriously vanished.

What happened to his things? Marta asked.

What things? The concierge replied contemptuously. There were no things.

Mona talked to the doorman, who found someone from maintenance, a blond boy half Marta's age and weight, who let her into the cages in the basement, where she found only a small drawing of a dog, one corner torn, and an unopened box of men's underwear, color blue, size medium, which the concierge had had no interest in.

Don't tell Mona, she told Gordon. She'll laugh.

I'll laugh, said Gordon.

You'd better not.

But Mona only snorted and everything went on as before, from breakfast through elevenses and drinks after dinner. The clients were served cheaper coffee and that was the end of Allan.

What happened to that dog picture? Mona asked one morning when the three of them were lunching on the patio in the shade of a large palo brea. A rabbit was making its way in stages through the cholla on its way home after a night of too much alfalfa.

No idea, Gordon said.

Not a topic for lunch, Mona said, biting off a bit of toast.

Marta pouted for a while. Keep the underwear, Mona said.

Gordon let it be known among his acquaintances and eventually Dido Makros turned up, presenting himself one cool afternoon. His well-tailored wine-colored roadster stood on the gravel of the semi-circular driveway and he and Gordon talked about edgy new artists until well into the evening.

Dido, no more hard-headed than he always had been, nevertheless got a better percentage of sales. In May of 2012, when Mona died, he and Gordon took over the gallery, renamed it Brisbane-Makros, and began to move into a different kind of art than that which Mona had wanted to represent. Marta carried on contentedly entertaining clients. On Thursdays she resumed hosting the old circle of bridge players, with the difference that she no longer had to clear up afterward herself.

Poets When They Are Grown Up

Autumn again. Fedya Volkoff began his season of small readings and hanging about wherever there was wi-fi. Tonight he was sitting in the Xtreme Bean with an empty espresso cup when a woman he knew — knew of — came in, so when she passed on her way to get a napkin and a plastic spoon he said hello.

Oh, hi! She said with e-mail brightness.

He invited her to sit at the counter with him. This counter was only about ten inches wide. Some stools were drawn up there, but with nowhere to fit under the counter people had to sit turned knee to knee.

You're the poet, she said. I heard you read a couple of weeks ago.

This was a surprise. As a poet, Fedya was not accustomed to being listened to.

This woman, whose name was Connie, he knew as the owner of a cleaning service employed by the better-off faculty, such as the woman who had been his friend Domenic's dissertation advisor. Until she died.

Died?

Well yes. He supposed. Died. Both of them, actually. That is, she and her husband.

After that of course, Connie — or was that the name of the business? — didn't clean there anymore.

How exactly, this Domenic, do you know me?

Well, she told me.

Who did?

Hanna — that is, Dr. Floyd.

I thought she was dead.

Well, yes.

An enigma. She let it lie.

You're Connie Anchor, he said, which he knew because he had looked into it.

Anker, she said.

She was annoyed. Fedya apologized, though he didn't know what for. Anchorwoman seemed about to leave, so he spoke his business at once.

I need a lawyer, he said.

What? I don't know any lawyers.

Yes you do.

Who are you?

I'm a poet, he said. It's my friend Domenic. He needs a lawyer. An inexpensive one that you know who is legal aid and can tell him what to do.

And what do you do? You're not even a grown-up.

Fedya winced.

I am Fyodor, that is Theodore, Volkoff: poet.

And what have you done, Sir Poet?

Nothing, Fedya said.

That's plain.

That is, published nothing. In actual fact I've written only a handful of poems which I use over and over like a superannuated preacher. I used to know one of those when I was a boy — still a boy — I worked it out. It was an epicyclic orbit you see, Ptolemaic. He had thirty of them, sermons… Ah, so. No, it's as you say, I'm not a member of any faculty. I teach nothing. Everyone, you know — poets and writers of all sorts from prize winners who are also ranked from grand down to the prizes given by village newspapers published once a week, usually on Wednesday for some reason — to the peasants who pass their wretched lives as adjunct English professors teaching introductions to things, and finally to the midnight security guards and the cubicles of the electronic degree mills — everyone who is a poet has at least a part of a room with a desk, or a table, and two chairs — even the virtual poet has that much — though not necessarily walls or windows, and at least one student entitled to be so called without respect to anything actually studied. People who like me are not poets because we have none of this and so no place, and being without place we are not poets. Hey, we should have plumbers like this. Not, thank god.

Connie Anker looked at him curiously, unaccustomed to being spoken to in such a way by a person she had never herself spoken to before.

Hey, she said. Did your dog die?

He smiled. It was not a restored smile, rather a pale one, a bit sickly.

So who are you really? she said, not unkindly. When you're grown up?

I'm a freelance software engineer, he said.

No.

Yes. But I am also a poet, always with a plan, a scheme which could remake the world into a thing of beauty. Which it is not. Now. I'm not in the business of apps and gadgets for smart phones or tablets or internet-connected refrigerators. I'm a transcendental software engineer in the same way that I might have been a poet, because I write software that does something and doesn't break while doing it, which everyone agrees really is software.

And this is the way you make a living?

No, Fedya admitted. I do triage or one-off development of a web presence for small businesses.

I thought so, Fedya, Connie said, for the first time addressing him by name. I hope your code doesn't work the way your mind does. How old are you?

Thirty.

Then we're the same age, more or less.

Well, I feel old. Transparent. When you are old there is no point in changing something unsatisfactory because when you are old nothing lasts. On Monday night I ran across this woman, whose name I believed was Anchor or something likewise reassuring, in a coffee shop. I stopped to chat, stopped her to chat, and now I am going home to question my whole existence. Home and existence being, like my status as a poet, after a fashion.

Fedya got the hiccups, and after a moment's disgusted astonishment Constance Anker left the Xtreme Bean without ever finding out about the lawyer.

And there was a pianist, a truly old man, a sort of demon or crossroads riddler, who now rolled up his music and went away, also.

Fedya's heart was beating as slowly and powerfully as an old motorcycle engine while it waited for the clutch to drop. The light changed. The bike went off, shedding its imprisonment. There was a bang and up ahead, and just over the horizon there rose a puff of blue smoke. Backfire, Fedya said to himself. Maybe it was not a good thing to be grown up?

And what on earth had happened to Allan? He had been gone five months now, fallen into the ocean and drowned, taking Fedya's livelihood with him, leaving him to repair stupidly written web-sites and setting up home wireless networks. What had he been doing behind Fedya's back to get his feet into a cement bucket?

Domenic didn't need a lawyer. Domenic was on his way to Hong Kong and Ven. Professor K.L. Dhammajoti PhD (Kelaniya), Glorious Sun Professorship in Buddhist Studies, bless his mudraic heart. It had taken a while. Over a year.

It was Fedya who had wanted the lawyer.

Maybe the piano man knew why. He had looked like one of those village elders who know everything.

And what was it with Fedya's ruse with Domenic? As Connie had seen at once, efficiency and directness were virtues for computer code but not so much in the other, poetic world. Despite his protestations to the Anchorwoman, Fedya felt himself to be competent in the coded world and a decent poet, if not a prolific or ambitious one. Poetry was twisty and indirect, and it was necessary to proceed accordingly.

A Small Business

Constance Anker, for that was her name and that
was how it was spelled, lived with a woman also
called Constance, though she spelled it differently.
Together they were a maid service, Connies'
Cleaners, which was handy since nobody ever noticed the plural apostrophe and they both could
claim to be The Connie when it was convenient,
though they looked nothing alike. Connie was tall
and thin with blond hair cropped tight under a do-
rag, one color for each day. Sunday was white for
no work. The other Connie was thick and short and
had long black hair which she kept in combs also
under a do-rag, really a dark blue turban. She
looked Hispanic, as she was, and this was getting
to be a problem because clients assumed she was
illegal and wanted to pay her less. When she re-
fused, some of them threatened to call — and here
there was some confusion. Some sort of police.
One actually did call the Sheriff, and Constanze
was put in jail overnight. In the morning Connie
showed up with a legal aid lawyer and Constanze's
American passport. They were going to let her go
anyway, of course, since holding her at all for an
identity check was illegal, the lawyer said..

Be glad you weren't arrested as a Sikh terror-
ist on account of the turban, he said. The lawyer
was fair-haired and younger than either Connie
and wore a white djellaba and was probably familiar with being shot at and detained.

Constanze Lourdes had been working up a
rage for quite a while. It was a slow rage. Do they

want marching in the streets? she fumed at Charles
when he brought her home — for Charles was the
lawyer's name. Do they want to destroy everything
just to keep the rubble for themselves?

All her life small epiphanies had been eroded
away to nothing by betrayals, cruelties, little fail-
ures and disappointments. She would make herself
over, begin again, and again be worn away to nothing. Now she had met Connie who had started a
business which had not failed yet, and lost twenty
pounds. Whether it was better to be angry or sui-
cidal was not yet clear. Stomach acid was starting
to back up into her throat, creating a rope of pain
in her chest. She was becoming as mean and unhappy as everyone else. Mass murders in movie
theaters and schools, atrocities in Syria, Sikhs
killed in church. Probably it wasn't called church.
The Depression and the depressed, the Elected and
the Downfallen, the rude, the philistine, the barbar-
ian. Constanze Lourdes spent her days washing
away grub and grime and germs, and leaving one
little orthogon of space, for a little while, clean.
Not purified, but a vision of it. She met a house
painter who said the same thing about his job. I
take off the old coat, he said, and put on the new
one, and it is now a house perfectly dressed and
creased for one night out and a date with a good
woman.

Houses are men, he said. Ships are women,
houses are men.

The young lawyer with the fair hair came

back, pro bonoishly, to see how see how Constanze was getting along. That wasn't it of course. His
hair was more than fair, it was almost white actually, his skin was translucent like a bathroom window, his eyes were as pink as a rabbit's. Constanze's own hair and eyes were black and her skin terra cotta, and the silly symbolism of black and
white wasn't lost on her, but she didn't care. They
were neither of them tall, nor skinny.

His name was Charles, he said. Charlie sometimes, what people call you when they don't know
your name. Luigi, Ivan — he skipped the Mexican
one diplomatically.

There was some small talk, small laughter.
There were pale smiles, barely lit. Still, even small
things were rare.

Later on Charles told her more about his job.
They were sitting at an outdoor table at a French
café located inside a glop of high-rise businesses
and a hotel at Camelback and 24th Street. They had
come for the croissants, which Charles said were
authentic.

And the other sort?

Industrial, Charles said. Frozen dough in muffin pans.

So these are hard to get? Constanze peeled off
a skin of pastry.

Three other shops I know of. Tempe, Scottsdale, north Phoenix.

You were going to tell me about the business,
Constanze said.

It was started, the business, Charles said, by Felix Kurz, a lawyer who, like himself, lacked the gravitas for commercial practice and the smoothness for a courtroom. Felix's appearance would have distracted the jury from consideration of his brilliantly original arguments. He himself, Charles, did not make brilliantly original arguments, but was only a factotum.

So why become lawyers in the first place? Constanze asked.

The intellectual challenge. Straightening out tangled thinking. And then there are idealistic lawyers, you know. Maybe you find that hard to believe.

Oh, I don't know. To clean things up, she said. A little bit, anyway. A little bit idealistic. So what's the matter with him, this Felix?

He doesn't say. A dwarf. Ugly as you can imagine, all mis-shapen. He has these terrible moods. Gets into rages, awful funks. He wears braces, walks with a kind of shuffle. He takes all kinds of pills. Always pills. You can hear him in his office, rattling his pills as he sorts them into his pill cases. He calls that Kalaha. Whatever that means.

Pain? Or a drug addict of some sort?

Charles shrugged. He doesn't say, he said.

Both of them peeled off another layer of croissant in silence, the subject of Charles's boss or perhaps mentor — Constanze couldn't say — drowned in the waves.

Charles reached out and delicately brushed

the back of her hand once with his fingertips.

The Triumph of the Will

Connie Anker was a cooler, more remote woman than her business partner. Commonly they paired their clients in the opposite way, so that Connie got the more outgoing ones, and Constanze the safer ones. That meant — sometimes — the never happy ones, always dissatisfied, full of regrets and sadness. So it fell to Connie to strike them off. Four de-commissioned so far — two boy stockbrokers, a middle-aged well-kept woman of indeterminate profession, and one of those women who had never recovered from her last pregnancy. She lived in an apartment littered with children's detritus and a husband's rinds and crumbs, but never a sight of any actual husband or child. Or herself. And she never liked what she got — something was not shiny enough which had been shiny five minutes earlier, something was out of place which had, for an instant, been tucked neatly away. The drapes were wrongly closed tight rather than left an inviting half-inch apart as they should have been. Inviting to what, or who, Connie never discovered.

The problem with the other three was mostly that they never paid.

Four people, Connie supposed, was not a representative sample. Just ordinary tightwads and schizoids.

Which reminds me, she said to Constanze

over dinner, though she didn't know why she should think of it now, are you still interested in that pale fellow in the burnoose?

Constanze nodded, her mouth full of spaghetti. Djellaba, she said, swallowing, but it still sounded like overcooked pasta. Connie smiled helpfully.

Connie's habitual appearance, manner, and expression made her seem the epitome of the icy blonde. This was useful for business — it made her hardnosed, or headed — emotional distance could imply cynicism and manipulation, but in her case the quality hardness meant incorruptible. And after all it was only a stereotype, and it was not difficult even for people whose skin had not been crusted over by too many hours beside the pool to sense the falseness of it. It was caution, that was all. She had learned to be careful.

Connie's best quality was loyalty, but she did not know it. Herself she thought fickle, so she expected everyone to be fickle, and so she was surprised when that poet she had treated so haughtily turned up on the street outside her apartment. She was looking impatiently for the right key on her ring when she heard a soft voice say her name and there he was at the bottom of the stairs, waiting. Flustered, she jammed the key too hard in the lock and rapped her knuckle.

Yes?

They arranged to meet at the neighborhood Starbucks not far away. Connie stowed her supplies and tools in her car in the parking garage and walked the four blocks to where this odd man had been, she learned, waiting most of the morning. They sat in the armchairs by the window in not yet companionable silence.

Yes? she said again, but before he could answer she got up to get two small coffees no room and a biscotti.

Did you want one? she asked, meaning the biscotti. Fedya said no.

I need a lawyer, he said after a time. You have one.

No I don't.

Can you recommend me? he went on, ignoring her denial.

What is this about? Why are you asking me?

Fedya took a breath. Your partner —

Business partner.

Knows Charles who works for Felix Kurz who is a lawyer.

I've never met him.

Don't be difficult, Connie.

Miz Anker.

Fedya inhaled a lot of air, let it out slowly, and began to hiccup. He pinched his nose and the hiccups stopped.

I know a man, he began finally. A woman he knew died. They arrested her husband. I think that's what they did. They think —

Who thinks?

Well, the police, I suppose. Maybe.

They're supposed to say, aren't they?

I don't know what they said. My friend asked me to find him a lawyer. They think he had something to do with it. That he was having an affair with her.

Was he?

I don't know. Maybe. He's a poor graduate student. Destitute. He needs a lawyer.

Student. Not too old for an affair with an old woman?

Thirty. Maybe thirty-five. How did you know she was old?

Guessed.

Connie sipped at her coffee, which was still too hot.

Does he have a name? she said. Your fatal young man?

Domenic.

Last name? And how do you know all this, um.. Your name again?

Fyodor. Fedya. I ask around. Everybody knows somebody who knows somebody. It's a closed loop. Recursive.

What's that, recursive? Fyodor.

Fedya. Never mind.

Persistent little beggar, aren't you?

No. Connie.

If you know his name why don't you just go? Kurz. Legal aid doesn't ask for references.

Fedya turned on her a whimpering beagled eye.

Roped into something, have you?

No. It's just —

OK, she said. I'll see what I can do. You probably know my phone number? Don't use it. I'll be working. E-mail me. You'll know that, too. A couple of days, she said, leaving her coffee which was still too hot and taking the biscotti.

But Domenic never turned up, of course. And Fedya got the lawyer he wanted.

Kurz

Felix Kurz was a twisted little man who looked as if he was meant to have been taller. He was squashed, with a wide face and mouth, a heavy jaw, and thick muscular fingers. His behavior was molded in a similar way — muscular, gruff, heavy-jointed. He was angry much of the time, which he and others put down to his dissatisfaction with the way of the world, the same attitude which had made him a lawyer to people in need of justice and unable to buy it. But the way of the world, to his mind, extended much farther. It took in the other animals, which he regarded as a mistake, plants (at best, an encumbrance), and perhaps the laws of physics. At any rate he often said that he would have liked to live in the time of the first humans so as to murder them all, rid the earth of a scourge, and have the place to himself for a while.

Much of this was only humor, but he was indeed an unhappy man who felt himself to be an arbitrary victim, like someone struck by lightning, the object of a retribution meant for someone else, visited by far too many afflictions to bear. And these feelings, along with an inadequate distribution of justice, did give him some sympathy with the world's benighted, though he did not often show it and rarely collected on it. Lent him some sympathy would be more accurate, in Charles's opinion.

Kurz was not unaware of the significance of his name. He thought he had some insight into the heart of darkness, a heart being an object which ought to have been but was not, or not any longer, found now just below his breastbone, obstructing the action of the valve which emptied his stomach. To be heartless improved his digestion, at any rate. The darkness at issue took the form of a profound pessimism, bordering on nihilism had it not been tempered with a simple love of the not living but not dead things of the world. And though he loathed the world as he found it, individual persons, rocks, saguaros, snakes (and so forth) were to be recused (for the most part) as having some prior entanglement with their own existence. These strange and secret feelings were hinted by his given name, Felix. He was thus a person of contradiction and conflict, the perfect lawyer, and impossible to bear for more than five minutes.

His assistant Charles, who he exploited unmercifully and often ridiculed for not being the color he should be, nevertheless guessed at Kurz's hidden qualities, though in the eight months he had so far worked for the man he judged them too well hidden to benefit anyone. If Charles had not have had other reasons to be here he would not have been.

Charles was himself a man of considerable empathy who frequently was able to tweeze out feelings that others could not. Kurz knew what Charles knew about him, and this unacknowledged bond Kurz regarded as a benign blackmail. This made him angrier than ever.

Nothing was as it should be. And now here was Charles with some penniless apprentice scholar accused of being a murderer, or at least an accessory to same. The authorities, whoever they were, had maliciously left the dead woman's husband alone for more than a year while the feckless lover chewed his fingers to bloody stumps from anxiety and dread, awaiting the incomprehensible hiss of the samurai's sword to flay him into a mass of undeserved pain.

Or something of that sort. Kurz was fond of hyperbole. That, too, was a useful quality for a man in his line of work.

At any rate, there was still some need of his services. This Domenic, the inquisitor saint which he certainly was not, combined with the bird of ill omen which he certainly was, Parra, an owl, was certainly too paralyzed to help himself, for now he too had disappeared.

Felix crossed his arms on his desktop, empty

except for a gel pen which he turned like a compass to point at Charles, and thrust his big head forward,

So, he said in his rumbling voice, who was he supposed to have murdered?

His dissertation supervisor.

Yes, we know that. By who supposed?

Charles gave over his information quietly and Felix agreed likewise not to ask Charles how he knew this about their ghostly client.

By name? Man or woman?

Hanna Floyd.

Unusually close relationship, that. Intense. He was sleeping with her, of course.

People said he was.

What people.

Her husband.

And what, Felix said, has happened to him?

We don't know. He's disappeared.

Felix faced the man who had escorted the shade of Domenic the Owl into his office and who was now waiting patiently and confidentially in the consultation chair on the other side of the desk. Charles the White. Behind him the door stood pointlessly closed.

The husband, Charles went on, has probably been arrested. Apparently arrested. At any rate, carried off. Somewhere. By uniformed men. Of course, no one asked them to identify themselves or show authority. No one seems to have cared.

Person is being held —

Unknown.

By unknown authority at a place unknown under unknown charges.

Yes, Charles said. This last March.

I see. And how was Mrs. Floyd murdered?

Unknown, Charles repeated with the lightest amusement. She was found dead one morning — over a year ago now — half dressed, apparently getting ready to go to class.

Found by who?

Whom. Her husband. They had separate bed-rooms. He had been out for coffee, which he usual-ly did mornings in order to avoid encountering her, and looked in to see why she was still there. Ap-parently there. Her car was there.

So rather than getting ready for work, Felix said, she might have been getting ready for bed. That leaves an opening of what, twelve hours? He turned to the absent Domenic. And you, he said, you miserable slime, evolved out of a cauldron of rotten soup and left on the parched rocks to die two billion years ago, what do you say? Alibi?

No, Charles said.

Felix paused for thought. Curious, he mut-tered, looking about the room before settling his gaze on the window behind him. Aside from a desk and two chairs the not very large room was bare. There was nothing on the walls, which were stained in several places with yellow damp. The agency's files were kept Elsewhere. Outside the window, only a few feet away, was another wall with another identical window. Between the walls was an alley just wide enough for a garbage truck which always stank of rotten meat.

The window in the wall opposite had never in Kurz's time been cleaned and the empty room behind it had waited years now for the unlikely return of Sherlock Holmes.

The shady, chiaroscuro Domenic was dismissed with a promise, feebly delivered, to see what could be done.

Acquaintances, Charles? Felix asked when the unincorporated Owl had gone.

I don't know.

Friends? Colleagues? Mother?

Unknown.

What do you know? Sir?

Nothing. Sir.

Which explains, I suppose, Felix mused with uncharacteristic quiet, why you are a student.

Charles shrugged off this canard. In the unilluminated room his stark face and dress glowed fluorescently.

Sentimental fool, Felix muttered, and turned to the window's darkly glass. Begone.

When Charles returned, Felix was standing just where he had been two days earlier, by the window, back turned to the door.

Well?

His disappearance, Charles said — Domenic's disappearance —

Unnoticed, Charles. We noticed that.

Charles had come to stand beside Felix, who now reached up to tug the cuff of his shirt. Charles bent and lifted him up — with surprising ease for such an etiolated man as Charles appeared to be — to stand on the window sill.

Where is he, then? Kurz said in a grating, pugnacious voice, his reddened eyes now on a level with Charles's. Charles stood his ground.

No one knows. The people I talked to are unlikely to know. Strange things happen all the time which are strange only because something is missing. There's a hole in the story.

Of course there is.

The bitterness in Kurz's voice did not escape Charles. Something is always missing, he said, almost spitting in Charles's face.

He hopped down from the window sill. From a lower drawer of his desk he took out a whiskey flask and poured into a smudgy glass, also retrieved from the bottom drawer, something which might have been either liquor or apple juice. Charles suspected it was juice and the whole pantomime was intended to satirize the hardboiled man which Felix Kurz certainly was not. Felix sat down in the yellow wooden office chair which must have been his grandfather's. Worked in a bank, 1925. Some small dusty town in Iowa. Felix put his hiking-booted feet on the equally yellow desk. Leaning back, puffed up like a miniature Nero Wolfe crossed with Spenser's eyes and the original Perry Mason's sneer, he drank off the brown liquid and poured himself another.

Metaphysical, he said.

I'll try to verify some of this, Charles offered.

Go for it, white boy, Felix said. Or whoever you are.

After Charles had gone out, quite cheerfully for now having something to do, Felix sat on. A sour expression crossed his face. Deliberately he had left Fedya Volkoff unmentioned, whose complicity was certainly not what it appeared to be.

Likewise this Connie Anker who recommended Felix to Fedya.

Bricolage. Some sort of cargo cult.

How It's Going to End

The coffee shop had been crowded that morning. The Man With No Socks had asked to share a table with a natty but surly man, who nevertheless agreed. The Man With No Socks had too many things in his hands. The coffee, which had slopped over onto the knee of his trousers, a plate with a raspberry bar and a fork — the fork fell on the ground — a pencil which he likewise dropped and a newspaper opened to the crossword puzzle. When he bent over to pick up the fork and the pencil he poured more coffee onto his newspaper. Everything together at last, he murmured. An incoherent apology. The other man was looking at his feet. Well, at least the shoes matched.

The man across the table hastily finished his bagel and went out. The Man With No Socks went on sitting, smiling a little stupidly. He tried to frown, but preferred his more habitual stupid smile. An elderly, frumpy woman asked to have the unoccupied chair. The Man With No Socks gestured his compliance and went on with his thoughts, dropping now one and now another, picking them up, puzzling over his now ruined crossword. Four-letter word for something. Smeared.

Mornings were often like this. Perhaps he ought to try another shop, but The Man With No Socks knew himself to be incorrigible and that it would make no difference. He wanted to be liked but he didn't much like himself or anyone else. This was a failing, he knew. He failed at many things. He did not understand the rules of propriety others set so much store by. He couldn't make small talk. He hated noise and loud voices. He was often flustered. He spent too much time by himself. All of these things were obstacles to being among people which he could no more overcome than he could overcome being tall. He stooped. He made an effort. A futile effort to stand upright.

But really, he always asked after working through this familiar sequence, what did it matter? He was only another rabbit.

People underestimate rabbits, he knew. They go about their business and keep quiet about it except for sex and death, which are after all also their business. They go to sleep if you turn them upside down. They can't help it. It seems an odd thing, but there it is. If you ruffle them behind the ears now and then they will sit on your lap for hours until you go to sleep yourself, which is hardly an odd thing. A long time ago they made an existential choice and they are not to be deflected from it by any means, which is a survival strategy of the herd and a plan of rapid breeding to replenish the herd in spite of everything — snakes, dogs, tularemia, eagles, bulldozers. Underneath their placidity rabbits are stubborn, profoundly pragmatic animals. The stubbornness ties them to the world, the pragmatism releases them from it. They are the zen masters of the animal kingdom. They know the answers to more cosmic riddles than any species alive, including the one about extinction.

III

ESTUARY

It was obvious to Felix by the time he returned to the office in the morning that the only thread in his hand was Domenic. Reaching up to put his key into the lock, he had already asked himself what had happened to the man and how he could find out in the face of a cosmic, perhaps metaphysical silence.

Metaphysical was a word he used often. Overworked, Charles said. But so much of Felix's work was overwork. Metaphysical work which was not going to get him the editorship of a law review. Waking and sleeping, Felix Kurz lived in a numinous, magical world of unresolvable mysteries. His job was to manufacture plausible stories about the goings on in this world. That was the work of reason. Writers, artists, musicians — these people did it all the time. He didn't see why a lawyer should be trapped in a mundane world of logic.

The door opened. Nothing had changed. There was still Nothing on the walls, Nothing on his desk, Nothing to be seen from the window. But something was different. He felt its presence as a blind man does. Felix paused in the doorway, suddenly cautious. The sound of the key in the lock, the clicking of the tumblers aligning, had been muffled.

And a smell.

Felix slid into the room. Its bareness could not hide anything material, any new thing not there last night. His eye drifted sideways to the closet. In the summer he wore no jacket, and in the winter he left it on the back of his chair. Possibly he had never once looked in the closet.

He opened the closet door. Charles fell out.

He was, Felix quickly discovered, only unconscious. The closet smelled strongly of what Felix now recognized as chloroform, remembered from childhood visits to a laboratory with experimental animals. He felt Charles's pulse. Regular and rabbity.

Felix opened the window. In the relatively clean air Charles began to revive. In half an hour he was sitting in Felix's small chair complaining of a menacing headache and wiggling uncomfortably on a child's seat.

He knew nothing, of course. One moment he was there, the next moment he was there. In between was imaginary.

What were you doing here in the night? Felix asked.

I had been looking into the people on our list, Charles said artlessly, holding out his hands palms up. I came back to leave you a note that I wouldn't be in today.

And here you are anyway. Wouldn't a text message have done?

I suppose.

Well?

I didn't think of it. I —

Didn't have your phone. Of course you didn't. Had you anything with you? Papers? A notebook?

No. They — whoever — took nothing. To take.

Felix muttered something annoyed. He pushed Charles out of his chair and sat down heavily, swiveling toward the open closet and then the open window. The chair creaked as if it, too, had been chloroformed.

Well, he said carefully. We'll concentrate on Domenic. Nix on the others. It's his ghost which we are committed to defend. His and now yours.

I looked into him some more, Charles said, unfazed by ghosts. Admitted to the art history doctoral program five years ago. Dissertation topic accepted 2010. Not long after this his committee chair died, the only man on the faculty who knew anything about Buddhism, the man who Domenic had come here to study under.

Man's a menace, Felix said. Killing off professors as fast as Bluebeard.

The day after Christmas.

Heart attack, I suppose. Too much Buddhist lamb and red wine.

So it was, Charles went on, grimly amused, that Hanna Floyd took his place, although she knew nothing of Domenic's work. She was a medievalist. Expert in church architecture. The closest she had gotten to India was Turkey. Oxiana, wherever that is.

Turkmenistan. Not Turkey.

And there was something about Copts, Charles added, but a growl told him not to pursue that. She wasn't assigned to his committee, he went on. She volunteered.

Means nothing, Felix said. They always do. What's more interesting is why, after the other one died, Domenic didn't move on. To Yale. To Mumbai. Why stay here?

There was talk of that. Of — um — encouraging him to... It was Dr Floyd who encouraged him to stay.

Did she, Felix said, musing, and then brightly: Oh ye of poisoned brain, how's your headache?

Worse.

So, Charles, where is this man-owl? Who is he?

Down in the alley there was some rattling around. Felix put his head out. A raggedy woman dumpster diving. Stepping back, he banged his head against the window sash.

Domenic had an apartment on 5th Avenue, across from Jaycee Park. Undergraduate at Berkeley. That's all I know so far.

Get that cleaning woman you're screwing into that apartment. Use some pretense.

Charles bit his lip, kept his silence, and went out. The steel door of the stairwell at the end of the hall closed with a discreet bang.

Now for the first time in several days Felix bestirred himself, and not only because the room's stink was making him woozy. His thinking was woozy at the best of times. But he didn't trust Charles — not, he admitted, a good recommendation for an assistant, but there it was. Charles was just not imaginative. He was a plodder.

So Felix went out to see for himself.

Art professor dies. Domenic hangs around, gets another one. That professor dies. Mysteriously. Now out of the program, Domenic still doesn't move on. The professor's husband disappears. Mysteriously, a year later. Domenic hangs around. Friendly poet hunts up a lawyer for him, just in case, and now at last Domenic vanishes. Mysteriously.

Metaphysical man in pursuit of owl.

There was remarkably little purchase on this man's life. There was no landlady to talk to, just a rental office in Phoenix. The only person in the department of art history with whom he had had any relationship at all was dead. He had had no social life. No one claimed to know him, no one claimed to have seen him anywhere. He did not own a car, perhaps not even a bicycle — that was stolen and not replaced, and for some reason this extraordinarily cautious and private man had chosen to go to the campus police about it even if, as he should have known, it would be futile.

Fourteen thousand graduate students in this school. How many of them led such lives? Poor, friendless, scrabbling away for years to get a degree in a subject they would come to hate and which would never pay them a living. Grown men and women in their thirties and forties reading hundreds of academic books and articles a month not out of curiosity but fear in that someone, and there would always be someone would sniff out some little corner of humiliating ignorance. Fourteen thousand anonymous, invisible people not wanted for anything but to make the shirtwaists and fill up the pin factories needed to provide half a dozen of themselves comfortable lives. They were the muddy pond water for the water lilies to float on for Monet to paint.

And then one of them disappears. What is to be done to find a man with no identity? About whom there is nothing more to be known than the clone number of the strain of white lab mice to which he belonged? That he bought milk and cookies at the corner market on Hardy. That he did not even own a cell phone. That probably the only thing of consequence that he did own was that essential laptop computer. Wherever he went the computer had gone with him even into oblivion. Nothing of himself had been left behind.

The Wrack
1

Charles came up with some background eventually. Childhood in Lodi, some high school almanac pictures, a newspaper article about his winning a Chamber of Commerce prize for a poster touting zinfandel wine. No one remembered him.

Not even his mother? Felix asked, acidly.

I don't know, Charles admitted. Dead, like all the rest.

But when Felix turned his attention to Hanna Floyd he made a small breakthrough. Most of the Floyds' neighbors lived too far apart to keep an eye on each other. However, one woman who appeared to have nothing to do but get botox treatments and pedicures had seen an "unusually slovenly" man who was a more or less regular visitor. Once a week perhaps he trudged up from the bus stop — such people do — do use the bus, that is — with a backpack and flip-flops and mussy black hair.

That would be Domenic. Of course he had every reason to be there, although Dr Floyd's office on campus would have been much more convenient for him. Except that, Felix found out from the department secretary, she rarely used it, and wouldn't even stop by for her mail. Admittedly, any paper mail was likely to be junk. But this scruffy man who did not belong in Paradise was the first sighting of Domenic. Of course, such information led nowhere and proved nothing but that the man had been alive at some time before he disappeared, which in this case might be useful to know. That he was alive.

There was nothing more to be learned of Domenic there — Allan sold the house when he moved, and the mid-town condo had now been emptied out as well.

2

The best, and it might prove only, informant was Marta, the gallery assistant during the time of Allan's partnership with Mona Magdalena and his one-time condo neighbor.

Mona had had no heirs, Marta said, crossing her legs with the long practice of someone who only wears skirts. Her legs were short and muscular, with the high calves which result from wearing heels. Just now she was dishabille in sandals, tartan, and a red button-down shirt worn untucked. The rest of her appeared to be as muscular and tight-packed as her legs. Felix thought that if they stood together she would be about his height and size, a comparison she obviously would not have liked. But it was she who gave Felix a seat from which his feet could reach the floor.

Marta could tell him nothing about the unforthcoming Allan Floyd, who disappeared two weeks after Mona died. More or less everything had gone to Gordon Brisbane except the actual gallery, which consisted of some paintings and drawings, some on consignment, computers, and a fungible reputation. Proceeds from sales, after working capital was set aside, had formerly gone into a trust fund which Gordon had never seen, nor knew the beneficiary. That was taken apart by the similarly invisible executor, leaving Gordon few liquid resources with which to rebuild. He and Marta now ran the gallery and lived quietly and peaceably together in an ex-urban desert house big enough for a family of eight. The house, Felix saw, was designed for entertaining, now forgone. A large part of it was this single room of irregular shape in which Felix now sat with Marta in one of its nooks.

Yes, Gordon said, passing through with a cup of coffee and declining to sit. There is now another investor, a collector named Theodore Makros who your man Charles brought in. With better taste than Allan's, fortunately. Fortunately he doesn't live here. Why Allan preferred to do so I never understood. Keep an eye on his investment, doubtless.

Gordon shifted his coffee cup to his other hand and closed his eyes a doubting fraction. He was trying not to notice Felix, whose taste in body forms was not of the best. Reminded him of Velasquez. A compliment, actually.

Allan was a suspicious man?

Allan was disinterested in everyone and everything. In this case I really think it was only that after a lifetime of it he was tired of living alone.

Gordon Brisbane's habitual party eye shifted to the side, always in search of someone useful to talk to. He excused himself and glided out to more private quarters.

Felix turned to Marta. What do you think?

She hesitated a long time before answering. If, she said finally, at hazard, Allan was tired of living alone why did he off his wife?

Felix ignored this suggestion for the moment, and said instead that perhaps he wasn't actually living with her — that is, together. That is, with.

I suppose not, she admitted, turning surly.

Felix had modulated his deep, grumbly voice but could change nothing else. He usually went away angry from interviews, and he knew it showed on his face, but they were necessary. Considering the unremunerated nature of his practice, Felix had always and regularly to ask for help, and he got it, but at a price.

Why, he said to Marta, do you believe that Allan Floyd murdered his wife?

I don't, she said, causing Felix to start. But it stands to reason. And some other people think so too, because they came and took him, didn't they?

She crossed her legs. It was evidently a rhetorical gesture, a mark of closure. Felix looked elsewhere. He took in the room they were sitting in. One wall was largely glass, with heavy sliding doors which opened onto the inevitable pool. There were drapes, now open, of something like damask. The décor of the room was largely Mexican, with red tiles, brightly painted furniture and doorframes. The art had been chosen accordingly. Through one door was a viewing room, very plain, now dark. Less conventional art was probably given space elsewhere. Felix looked again at the pool. Beyond the fence was open desert, just barely groomed, with its coyotes, wild dogs, rabbits, javelina, possibly a bobcat, mice, snakes, burrowing owls and cactus wrens, roadrunners, Gambel's quail all intact. Behind glass, an immense diorama.

Marta, he thought, did not care for the view, or indeed anything which might be called beautiful. For that matter, neither did Felix, being so excessively ugly himself. Marta was, like him, simply practical, pragmatic and utilitarian down to the bones. Heavy-boned, again like himself. Not likely to break.

What sort of woman was she? Hanna Floyd, he said, to clarify the question.

I never met her. Allan said nothing about her, but it was easy to see he didn't like her, and that he hadn't gotten anything from her for years.

Sex, you mean.

Marta nodded, looking at Felix as if surprised a person like him would know what that was.

What did he do, then.

She shrugged. Nothing, I think. Did without. He was good at that.

What about you?

She stiffened, but then took his meaning finally and relaxed. No, she said. He never made a pass. The soul of a gentleman, she said, scornfully.

He didn't talk about his wife's student Domenic?

As a matter of fact, he did. Assumed they had been getting it on whenever he was out, except that he was hardly ever out so they must have been doing it in her bedroom while he was in his office at the other end of the house.

A big house.

They're all big.

He was jealous?

No. He didn't like her enough for that. It was more like an insult. And of course he would wonder what they did that she would never do with him. They all do, don't they? It was hard to imagine why they got married in the first place.

Did he tell you this?

Uncrossed legs.

No. He said some things, I made up the rest. It's how I would feel.

Crossed legs.

Felix stood up to go, working as usual to catch his balance when his weight came firmly onto the floor.

You never met her, you said, he remarked as she was showing him out through a foyer as big and almost as bare as his office.

No.

It was true, they were the same size. But differently formed. Felix was long-waisted, so they did not match at the hip, and she had the longer arms. His head was bigger and his mouth wider and his eyes closer together. In mind they were one, irritable and unhappy, though her unhappiness was kept, Felix guessed, in a kind of jewelry box hidden from thieves under a professional bed.

Felix did not bother to challenge her. He knew by now from Dido Makros, who had more than once brought along Karen McAdoo at a time when he was only a prospective buyer, and then from Karen that Hanna had more than once been asked to authenticate some painting which she knew nothing about. And that Marta once said to Hanna, in Karen's hearing, that Karen was a shameless opportunist, which Felix thought sourly was something she would know about and was probably true.

3

It's wonderful, Felix said to Charles, how these people deal every day with things which they know nothing about. There's not even a pretense that they do. It's all nothing but book-jacket blurbs and sock-puppet reviews.

What?

When the book reviewer hasn't read the book. You're a cretin, Charles. What else have you turned up? Tell me those three women were all in bed together.

They were, in a sense.

All prostitutes, you mean.

Well, no. Except metaphorically. An artist, a professor, a gallery hostess. They were in a position to, that is to say —

I see. Gordon?

A blind eye. It all stopped when Makros came in.

It would, Felix said, rubbing up the back of his head, pushing the hair forward and causing it to stand out in two horns above his ears. Makros is a simple man who would have been horrified and blown the game. His money was worth more than any petty fraud might have been. What about Allan?

A narcissist. Corruption didn't concern him, except as regards his wife's — um.

Domenic?

A simpleton. A poor Makros. I think the Doctor was keeping him quiet with a few easy perversions.

You're sordid, Charles. You have a perverted mind.

Charles shrugged. The world is ugly and sordid, he said, causing Felix to give him a long, squinting stare.

Surely Domenic wasn't a real danger to her. To anyone.

Probably not, Charles said. She was doing it for fun, mostly. That's how these things work, isn't it?

Constanze cut you off, Charles?

This time Charles gave Felix an angry glare, and the staircase door slammed to with a somewhat less discreet bang.

After a time, Felix scrounged a scrap of paper and a pencil out of one of the desk drawers and drew some circles and line on it. The pencil point came to rest here and there, where he made notes in a miniscule hand.

Charles's hypothesis was nonsense. Any fiddling there had been with the provenance of the gallery's paintings would have had to take place before Hanna's death in April, eighteen months ago, long before Karen attached herself to Dido. Karen was merely a potter. Without Dido she would have had no entrée.

Except that Karen had been invited to that gallery opening where the disastrous Incident of the Water Glass …

4

Charles was telling a story, though. Some sort of story. But not that story of fraud and connivance — not that connivance. What did this have to do with being gassed and stuffed into a closet? Some kerfluffle. Some caution. What business could a colorless man in a djellaba be doing?

And who on earth would think it worth their while to search a poor dwarf's empty office and mug his empty-pocketed assistant?

Felix doubted he had ever exchanged a civil word with Charles. The man boiled with resentments, probably. Did any of these people actually like each other? The poet seemed to want to. The Connies apparently got along. Makros moved too slowly. By the time anyone got to like him he wasn't there yet. Mona was simply dead. Domenic had probably gone to Mumbai after all, after one of those Kama Sutra thingies backfired.

Brisbane. Not exactly a crook because he

didn't need to be. This Portland person nothing but a troublemaker. Marta merely expedient. McAdoo — both of them — an accident. Feckless Fedya.

Who did that leave?

Allan Floyd, ab initio.

Charles the Craven, amicus ignotus.

Constanze Lourdes, cognoscere clandestinus.

The phrase diplomated carrots was running through Felix's mind. What did that mean?

In school Felix had been made to take Latin because that was the only language option open to the unstudious. In retrospect, he had worked out the logic of it, which was that if you were not on the academic track you were free to study something useless. Felix had not studied because he hadn't needed to. The Latin teacher was a soft portly lady of indeterminate old age. She hadn't cared who learned what but managed to keep thirty future unemployables stupefied with her Circean voice. It was the only civilized course Felix ever took.

He swiveled around and around in his squeaky chair like a restless child. He looked at the half-open door and then the half-open window. He looked at the closet, the ceiling, the pencil shavings on the floor...

Who uses a pencil anymore? Besides Felix Kurz, whose pencil shavings —

And what was it Floyd actually did for a living? Did anyone know? Did it involve pencils? Unlikely.

Whatever that business was, it was something to do with ones and zeroes. The poet was a man of numbers. Charles was handy in that way. Who else?

Who, for instance, was Anker before she was Connie?

Felix stopped spinning in his chair and went out. The identity of Connie Anker was something he could deal with. The other stuff, which once he would have referred to Charles, he could not. Yet.

Felix got the paper on Connies' Cleaners. Licensed and incorporated in 2009 without the apostrophe. Her clients came to her by word of mouth, referrals. There was no advertising. An e-mail address which came off the license application. Felix googled the business but found initially little interesting other than it was a common business name. There were Connies Cleaners everywhere. What was not advertising or irrelevant was complaints, the usual complaints about the usual things: late, slovenly, thieving.

Many pages down in his browser output Felix came across one of these complaints which seemed promising, but the links backward and forward went nowhere. Felix wrote down the griper's name for more old-fashioned research.

When he tried Connie herself what turned up was what he ought to have expected. There were thousands of Connie Ankers in the world, not counting sobriquets, pet names, and mis-spellings, a great many obituaries and other doings and not doings from local newspapers. There were tens of thousands of photographs — family reunions, new babies, graduations, drunken parties. To a secretive dwarf it was overwhelmingly shameless and sad.

Drifting through the pages and pages of Connies, Ankers, and variants, Felix noticed a few pictures which were more than ordinarily shameless. He pulled down the images query, turned off the safety, and typed in "Anker" — this produced an amazing variety of weirdness, a lot of it to do with ankles, and of course the plethora of seafaring decorations. He fiddled with the search terms but finally concluded this enterprise was only an excuse for some ogling.

He tried Facebook tags, but it was the same ocean of humanity. There were also not surprisingly dogs and cats named Connie, various objects including a dildo, men, football teams —

And Connie Anker herself. In some of the photographs there was a man busily violating her, but his face was hidden.

At some time in the past Connie was outed. Felix closed the cover of his laptop, his eyes narrowed with speculation and his wide mouth tight shut, lips pulled into a straight whitened line.

Returning to the original inquiry concerning the identity of the unhappy client, Felix found that there were ten possibilities nearby. Starting with the closest ones, he retrieved public records, from which he gleaned telephone numbers, and by the simple expedient of calling these numbers and asking whether it were Connies' Cleaners he quickly found one who knew who that was.

I was given this number, Felix said. I'm looking for a cleaning service.

Well, don't.

I beg your pardon?

The man's voice was light and edgy. Felix said he was looking for references.

For what?

The cleaners. Is it reliable.

No.

They don't seem to advertise anywhere, Felix complained. How did you find them?

A friend of mine used them.

Can you give me a name?

Look, who the hell is this? Larry Joiner told me. House on Ash.

It was good enough. Over several days Felix traced a network of less disgruntled customers, from whom he learned that Constanze had come in around April of 2010. The earlier references described her as inexperienced and distracted, slow to speak when spoken to, but good at the work.

Didn't answer to Constanze, Felix muttered, because that wasn't her name.

Clients from 2009 thought Connie had been angrier, more likely to take offense, than she became later on. Most of them stuck with her about eighteen months. When Felix asked why they left her it was because they'd moved.

Like across the street. A cleaning lady with attitude. Who cares what the cleaning lady thinks?

Quite a few people do, apparently. Aside from wanting to know who it is you're giving the key to, the cleaning lady is like someone you meet on an airplane. You get home early from work, you're tired and discouraged, the cleaning lady is doing the dishes. She's a nice-looking woman in her thirties, trim and fit, wearing a purple do-rag over short blond hair. She's easy to talk to. You lean against the kitchen counter, briefcase still at your feet, and tell her about your day. This is not going anywhere. You're not going to ask her for anything other than to finish the dishes. You'll never see her again. You talk. She tells you things like how to get wine stains out of rugs and that you need some new underwear and asks where you work out. Why not? The most she'll ever see of you is a sticky note on the cupboard door saying don't come in after Saturday. Your money is in the key box in the foyer. You don't take pictures.

Felix surmised that whatever Connie Anker had been doing before 2009 the outing had put a stop to it. A business in the shadows like a maid service had been a new option — unseen, low profile, word of mouth. And then there was Connie Lourdes to front for you just in case.

But the Lourdes woman had a past, too. There was no record of her anywhere before she turned up as Connie version 2, some bugs fixed and better security.

Connie Anker's office was a room in her

apartment in an unusual porticoed house in a small neighborhood, the only part of town to date from before 1946. This office consisted of a land-line, a desk with a single file drawer, an appointment book, and a pencil — everything portable or erasable. There was a mullioned window, now cranked completely open, and a swamp-cooler vent slumbering in the ceiling. There was a cup of tea, but Felix wasn't having any.

You recommended me to Domenic Parra, he said. He never showed up.

Went to finish his degree somewhere else, Connie said. Her voice was light and pleasant. She was fiddling with the teacup and an empty saucer like an ex-smoker who doesn't know what to do with her hands.

So I supposed. Allan Floyd was a client of yours. His wife was Domenic's dissertation chair.

Yes.

So you would know.

Should I? People don't tell the maid stuff like that. I don't keep track of the ex-students of ex-clients. More tea? she asked, perhaps impish, perhaps something more sharply edged. The tea was in a thermos. She poured another cup for herself and tipped in some milk and a dusting of stevia. Outside, some yelling children were going home from school. A breeze had sprung up out of the mid-afternoon as it often did early in October when the summer heat was dying. Connie turned slightly in her seat to close the window.

It was Fedya Volkoff, she said. I never in my life met this Domenic. Fedya came to me. Wanted my help.

How do you know Fedya then?

I don't.

Felix waited for her to go on, waited for the explanation which he already knew.

He knows Charles. Charles is courting my partner. The other Connie.

Felix exploded with laughter which in his voice sounded like a bass drum. Courting? What an antique idea.

Charles is an antique person.

Charles is a fool. He'll get nothing.

A look of speculative guesswork passed between them like the odor of the green tea. Fedya, he said, was acting for himself, of course.

Connie admitted to this with a slight turn and dip of her head.

And what does Fedya Volkoff want with legal aid?

I have no idea.

Well, Felix said heavily, with a sigh like the last of an old inner tube. That's not so, is it? Fedya is in business with a man you know, who is in the same business as you were, who you know because four years ago he published some pictures of you on the internet. Perhaps he's beginning to worry about that. He wants some way of keeping track of you. He asks Fedya to arrange it. And so we have this charade about the always-was irrelevant

Domenic Parra and the rest of it.

Connie slowly spread her long fingers on the desktop. The skin was beginning to roughen from the work she did. Her nails were unpolished but immaculate with a translucent gleam.

What was your work before those pictures came out, Connie?

That doesn't matter. I couldn't do it afterwards.

Did you know about them? The pictures. At the time.

Some. Two. He asked to make them. I agreed.

And the rest?

No. I suppose he had hidden the camera somewhere.

Was he going to sell them?

Hah! Wrecked the merchandise by putting them out for free, didn't he?

Why would he do that, Connie?

Says he didn't. Says they were on a flash drive he lost. Was stolen.

And you don't believe him.

No.

Plans?

Wait.

Connie's eyes drifted away to one side and then snapped back to meet Felix with a flash of venom and anger, a flash like an old press photographer's camera, with a pop and a little crackle. She reached back to close the window a little more.

Felix wiggled off his chair and stood up. Connie followed — on her feet she was about twice his height. It would not be the first time a woman made an obscene remark about this, but Connie let the opportunity pass. Nothing more was said. Felix made his own way out.

5

So there were three of them in it: Allan, Fedya, and this unknown person — Felix suddenly realized he was assuming this unknown person was a man. The man in the photograph. She had let him think that. And Felix now cautioned himself not to suppose he had heard the whole story, or even the right one.

So far Felix's construction of the situation had been mostly guess. Connie had helped to move that into the world of trusses and rivets. And so it was worthwhile to go on.

Charles did not think so.

We have other things to do, Felix. This business was phony from the start. We do legal aid. Pro bono stuff. We're lawyers. After a fashion.

Not after a fashion, Charles.

We're not detectives, anyhow. This whole business of Domenic Parra was phony from the start. Where's the crime? Where's the victim? Where's the tort? This is all morbid speculation. All you have done is to uncover some old injustices better buried.

Connie Anker doesn't think so.

It's not your business, Felix. You're meddling as always.

Hanna Floyd is dead.

Actually, that's a hypothesis. Allan Floyd says she is. Says he says she is. Common knowledge says what Allan says. Said. All roads to that village are closed.

Yes. Isn't that peculiar.

Charles clapped his hands in frustration.

How are you getting on with the short Mexican?

Charles only glared.

Connie Anker says you're doing a courtship.

What of it?

Nothing of it. Carry on. I was wondering whether I can continue to count on your services.

Yes, Charles said cautiously. With no guarantees.

Agreed. Now there's a third man in this.

Who?

Unknown. He's the man who outed Connie — that is, published compromising photographs of her on the internet. We need to find out who he is.

Why? Compromising?

Cunts, you've heard of those? Fucks and sucks. That sort of thing?

Charles modestly brushed some dust from the sleeve of his djelaba, a garment which Felix always thought looked like a plastic raincoat.

Those pictures came from somewhere, Felix

said. Can we find out where?

In theory, Charles admitted. But you'd need access to some proprietary servers and history which you are not going to get without a major hack.

OK, so at the other end. Connie says she agreed to two of them. Where did the others come from?

Hidden camera.

You're very sure, Charles.

It's the easiest way. Why look for harder explanations? Charles was still standing because there was nowhere to sit. He shifted his feet with impatience. Finally he chose to sit on the windowsill, which put him uncomfortably close to Felix, and he politely edged away.

Open the window, Charles. You'll have more room. Besides, you might fall out.

Sighing, Charles opened the window. Traffic and garbage came storming in.

You're thick with Constanza, Charles. Want to talk to the other one?

The other who?

Connie.

No.

Why not?

Connie plays the cosmopolitan, Charles said, but she's not so accommodating. We don't get on.

Charles, with your famous empathy I'm surprised to hear there's anyone you don't get on with. Aside from me.

Charles found some more dust on his sleeve. The slight breeze through the open window lifted some of the very lightweight cloth. He kicked his heel against the wall where there were a number of dirty streaks from Felix's climbing on it.

So Felix said he would do it himself, but he never got the chance. Two days later Constanze told Charles that Connie had taken the few things from her office, leaving behind the computer and the files with the business records and the client list, and walked out. At least, Constanze assumed she had walked. She woke up and found herself alone in the apartment. By the end of the day people were calling in. And that was that.

Next to go was Fedya, this time on Charles's report. And Charles drew Felix's attention to the murder of an economic advisor to the governor. The man was found dead in the afternoon the day before. Found by his girlfriend, who had let herself in with her own key. She called the police, but by the time officers arrived she was nowhere to be found. At present the cause of death was unknown.

And then the day after Charles himself disappeared. In his case, however, he re-appeared a week later, also dead, again in Felix's closet. This time the cause of death was easy to ascertain — he had been chloroformed — and there was a note pinned to his shirt. Perfidia.

Felix didn't bother to examine the pin.

Probably turned herself back into Leslie, he muttered.

Felix Kurz sat down in his small chair behind his small desk and put his feet into the empty file drawer, after first getting out the flask of whiskey. He poured himself a glass of this. As he drank it, he looked out the window at the building opposite, with the window which had never been opened. His eyes being at only the height of the window sill, Felix could see only the top of the window. He thought about lobbing the empty whiskey bottle through the glass.

Then he stopped thinking and did it. A few pieces of glass went into the alley, the rest inside. He could hear the bottle bounce on the floor and strike the wall opposite with a dim thud.

Felix took a pair of binoculars out of the desk.

Empty. It was hard to see anything. He thought he saw a glimmer of cobwebs.

He put the binoculars back, returned to his small chair, stuck his feet back into the file drawer, and looked over his shoulder at the magic closet.

6

Felix Kurz was restless. He had nothing to do — business had dried up, as everything does in the desert. In the desert there is little or nothing to be called leaves. The lifeways of the indigenii were spines on the naked branch, extracted from the Old Ones by study and struggle. To exact — extract — information from the desert of dry intimacy, a leafless people struggling to live, is never ending. But of struggle there is an end. The sand is strewn with the corpses of failure.

What had happened to all these people? Hanna Floyd, professor of artful history, who died for no reason whatsoever. Allan Floyd, made to disappear by some not very threatening men — almost invisible in fact. One by one the rest of them — Domenic the Owl, student of mudras, Fedya the poet-programmer, Connie Anker the Naked One, Constanze-Lindsey Lourdes Stein-Davis the many-named, Chas the Dead, Charles the Dead, plus a host of Others, their stories told, were now never to be heard from again.

Was this something metaphysical? Was there some old Noah at work behind the mountain, building a metaphysical boat? Soon Felix Kurz, destined to be drowned in a spiritual flood, would be sucked down to the root of the world, Prospero's powers gone. But Caliban was still in chains, and Ariel unfreed.

Felix had gone up to the top of South Mountain to get above all that, to the shelter at the top where he was accustomed to go at these times of confusion and dread. Now he jumped off the stone bench on which he had been sitting and began to pace the walls.

What a hash of tropes — dry, wet, embodied, disembodied, up, down, light, dark, floating, sinking, crippled, diminished, puffed up — a hash he had made of this story. He had given himself to this obsession like a fish with an existential quandary. It was as if all the other fish had all crawled out of the ocean and flippered away somewhere, leaving him behind. Obsessed by the need to follow, by the illusion that he had been left behind, he had failed to notice that Charles, pale Charles, lover of water, sun-shy Charles, had betrayed him.

White, light-allergic, rabbit-eyed Charles in his bloodless djellaba. Chump in habit, underestimated sacrifice, a tiny bit of the World Soul gone.

And with Charles, gone the business Charles had brought in, and so the office was now empty and Felix had discovered a contempt for his always-empty office, devoid even of the inanimate, and likewise a contempt for his newly-empty existence, and he did not go there anymore. He was a fish cast by a storm onto the beach, a fish in the desert, in need of water, which in confused desperation begins to wriggle and crawl in the wrong direction.

What, after all, had really happened to Charles? Why was he dead? Why was anyone living in the first place? Felix lived — he lived down below in three small rooms on 7th Street in south Phoenix, a poor Hispanic neighborhood not far from South Mountain. Overhead on that mountain was a high place, a lookout. That was where Felix was now, pacing with the rolling gait of his short legs around the walls of an adobe shelter.

Sometimes he stopped on the north side, looked down on the ragged houses and dusty empty lots where he lived unnoticed, northward toward the baseball stadium and the airport and nest of government buildings where his office was, where he was a furtive but noticeable presence, and beyond to the taller buildings of midtown where he never went.

Sometimes he stopped on the east side to look down on the town of Guadalupe where he had once lived, a mixed Yaqui and Mexican place where some people still cooked over wood fires in their front yards where they gathered in the evening for food and beer. But Guadalupe was becoming prosperous and the place Felix had known was fading.

To the south and west lay the spine of the Estrellas, blocking the view. Hidden behind this ridge, to the south, lay the suburb of Ahwatukee, squeezed between the mountain and a reservation now also becoming prosperous. Casino money. Felix never went there either.

He was without business or obligations. He was a fish who aspired to be a creosote bush, one of the oldest living things, with sunless connections everywhere. All creosote bushes are related, somehow. What seems to be an individual bush is actually a concession to the desert — a sacrifice sent up into the air like the nun who is selected to leave the purity of seclusion in order to transact the still-necessary business of the convent.

7

Kurz had decided to find out what had happened to Charles the Dead. He had decided to harry the harrowed.

The first thing to do would ordinarily have been to locate Constanze, if he had had any idea of how to go about that. She was down there somewhere, he felt sure, in that desert wilderness of three million people where he mostly never went.

Felix's eye turned to the northeast, to one of the University's four campuses, thinking of Ashley Portland.

And it was thus: Ashley begat Dugan and Dugan begat Chas and Chas begat Connie and Connie begat Constanze and Constanze begatted Charles and so on around them all and back to Ashley, one more generation than the canonical seven and two extra degrees of separation.

One way or another, Ashley knew them all. The people of Mona Magdalena's gallery where she once worked — Gordon Brisbane, the solely-named Marta, the Maecenas Dido Makros and his predecessor of the deep pockets, Allan Floyd, and so around again to Hanna, Domenic, Fedya — also known as Fyodor that is Theodore or, familiarly, Dido but not, in fact, Dido — Connie the First and Connie the Other to Charles. McAdoo to Makros. Connie to Chas.

But Dugan was fled, Chas was dead, Connie was in hiding, Constanze was at least three other people, Mona's heart had failed her after so long and Gordon wasn't paying attention, feckless Fedya forgotten, Hanna vanished, para-Parra now moored elsewhere, lovelost Makros, no love lost Karen and now Ashley again. Roads blocked, rails twisted, justifications disputed, time and paradise and salvation lost, alternative worlds unvisited, sins unforgiven. All all. Except Ashley Portland. And Felix knew how to find her.

What he didn't know was what he wanted to know.

Felix cornered her two days later about nine o'clock in the evening in the pit next to the art building where she and another woman had cracked a kiln and were beginning to unload it. The evening was cool, and the pale warmth of the open kiln invited him forward. On the way there, he moved to one side and leaned against the kiln wall. There were not many pots in the kiln for most of them were bigger than he was.

I want to talk to Constanze Lourdes, he said.

Who is that?

Felix kept his silence for a while. Two more big pots, the last of them, came out. They looked like lamp bases. Lumpy. Disfigured.

She has also used the name Lindsey Stein, he said.

Student?

At one time. Political science or something.

And what do you want to talk to her about. Mister Kurz.

My partner Charles, who is dead, knew her.

Can't help you. I don't think I should bother asking you how you got down here. I imagine the gate was unlocked.

She seemed to think he might have walked under it. Felix said nothing. It was not a strategy — he simply had nothing to say.

And your Charles?

The other woman finished shelving the newly fired ware and came over to look on. She was wearing clay-spattered jeans and a raggedy gray hoody. A medallion or amulet the size of her fist was hung on a heavy chain around her neck. Her tawny hair was pulled back into an untidy bun. A woman who knows a great deal, Felix guessed by the look of her eyes. .Someone good, useful to know. By contrast, Ashley was scrawny, long-necked, a woman all wires and steel, and probably not good to know.

Karen McAdoo, he said, not wanting to provoke a confrontation by keeping his silence any longer.

What a lot of names. Mister Kurz.

She took a light jacket from a nearby table and put it on, preparing to go.

Karen, she said, is close to a man named Makros who bankrolls the gallery where you used to work. So you will know Gordon Brisbane.

Ashley's close-set eyes lent her a natural sneer. It was only necessary to let them drift half shut, accompanied by the faintest lifting of one corner of her mouth.

Gordon, she said, is undoubtedly cognizant of some business involving Charles and some confederates. I want to know more.

Why don't you ask him?

I prefer to ask you.

Ashley was also a small woman, and Felix was probably the only man she had ever been able to look down on. For his part, Felix had long ago given up these showdowns. His comical appearance made him only appear beseeching or petulant, while any display of toughness turned his grotesque form into that of an angry wind-up toy. His usual defense was a show of cynicism. But this time, some unconscious genius urged him to an approximation of simple curiosity and on his wide toad's mouth a smile of something like kindness.

The combination was successful. Ashley finished shrugging on her own jacket, picked up a scruffy messenger bag, and indicated the stairs with a jerk of her head.

There's a Starbucks not too far, Felix said. I'll drive. I'm in that lot just across the street from here.

I'd rather the Rúla Búla, she said. If you're buying.

All right, then.

I don't suppose you want to walk. It's only a few blocks.

Ashley skipped up the stairs, waited for him at the top, and the two of them set out. Felix ordinari-

ly didn't like to walk any distance. He felt it made
him look ridiculous, trotting along on his short legs
like a Chihuahua. They came out onto Mill Avenue, now at ten o'clock gone largely indoors, and
turned toward the river. The pub proved boisterous
and noisy. They found a quieter place in a corner
of the dining room and asked for two pints and
some fish and chips.

You didn't get on with Gordon Brisbane, Felix said, and took a long drink of beer. He intended
to have several more. There was a small competi-
tion for the chips.

When Ashley started to talk it was clear that
she knew everyone after all.

About Dido Makros, she said, pay no attention. He's an insecure and lonesome person who
buys affection. Karen McAdoo's link to Hanna
Floyd is more important. Or would be if there was
one. Gordon might know about that. Probably he
doesn't. Probably he oughtn't. Probably he's a
snake.

Was it Mona, or the gallery, or only Gordon
you disliked? Or was it only that you wanted to go
back to actually being an artist?

Ashley waved off these questions, but after a
moment she decided they were worth answering,
and to Felix was revealed how little of this internal
deliberation showed in her face and manner. He
ought not trust her. Her opinions were going to be
hard to believe. Possibly more easy to confirm.

You need to ask Marta, she said.

About Gordon's being a snake, or Karen and Hanna, or what?

Those things.

About fucking the customers?

Mona had nothing to do with that, Ashley said, allowing some ferocity to escape with these words. It didn't happen. Maybe Gordon thought it did, or ought to. Dido was a collector before. He knows what to do. Allan didn't.

And what about Marta? Who is Marta, besides Allan Floyd's baggage?

Ashley shrugged, and Felix twitched with despair. A waiter came by and took an order for two more pints. A well-muscled man in a tightly fitting t-shirt, curly red hair and beard, only lacking the pack of cigarettes rolled into his sleeve. Too old to be a student — or would have been in Felix's time.

And Constanze? Felix asked when the waiter had gone.

Her name is Lindsey Hilliard and she's no more Hispanic than my cat. That's all I know.

Your cat?

What cat?

The waiter's return with the beer cut off this nascent hostility. Like all good waiters, professionally imperturbable to the disparity between Felix and his companion. Felix the Unfelicitous and this unlikely, unkind woman.

Felix looked about while he waited, sipped his beer, smiled at the pub's dark ambience which reminded him of graduate school. Every student of any sort, he had always thought, was entitled to be a member of a pub, and one dark enough to sit in a corner and talk about dark things. In Felix's day there were no women at these — well, what to call them?

I thought her name was Stein, Felix said. Lindsey Stein.

Might have been.

A silence passed.

I don't know, Ashley spoke up suddenly, about Marta. She might. She's a jumped-up cleaning woman who keeps the books and locks up at night. She knows nothing about art. What she and Hanna had to talk so much about is a mystery. You know about mysteries, Mr Kurz the detective.

Charles suspected some sort of fraud —

That's crap, Ashley snapped. Allan brought them both in. No need for complicated explanations.

She took a long drink and swallowed with a new little, complacent smile. Again, Felix sensed the depth of artifice in this woman.

Perhaps, he said, they recognized each other as prisoners.

Ashley snorted.

About Allan, then, Felix said, happy to strike out in a new direction.

What about him?

He was behind some scheme to bilk — that is, with Fedya Volkoff and Chas — apparently a gov-

ernment connection was needed, and Chas was that
— and this group brought Charles into the scheme
for some reason. As a tame lawyer perhaps. I have
the impression that this was how Allan lived. How
he made his money. How did he?

No idea.

Come on, Ashley.

Look you, I wasn't there in Allan's time. I
didn't see any suspicious men with three-day
beards and bulges under their coats. Probably. Allan Floyd was as much a snake as Gordon. I
wouldn't be surprised to learn that the mob —
some mob or other — had offed his wife to en-
courage les autres. Not that he would have cared.
He didn't care about Marta and he didn't care
about Limpdick or whatever his name was and I
doubt he could be encouraged and yeah, it was
probably the mob who took him away in the night,
don't you think?

So how was Hanna murdered, then?

Poisoned semen, Ashley said with a smirk and
looked down into her beer glass, again empty.
With her finger she traced a non-existent name
carved into the dark wood of the table by a long-
ago student.

I think, she said, your idea of a scheme — or
Charles's idea — is as stupid as the other one.

What other one?

Ashley shrugged negligently.

There was something going on, surely, Felix
said.

Nuts.

There's always something going on, Ashley continued. It usually involves sex or money. The mob didn't off Chas. Connie did it for revenge, as soon as she could hop the country and start a new life somewhere under the name — never mind that. And took Fedya with her. I think —

I think that's lurid, Felix said.

More than your conspiracy theories? Don't you think there are too many dead people here?

Yes, I do. And when there is something out of the ordinary there has to be something going on. Is that right? An explanation. You put two things next to each other and you say they must be related somehow, and this is the somehow.

She pushed their two beer glasses together, one half full and the other slightly smeared with foam.

Look! she said, mischievously. They're in love.

Ashley beckoned to the waiter, who had looked in from the bar to check on them. She held up two fingers.

Felix demurred. None for me.

Nonsense. You want a passel of little beer glasses. I know you do.

Ashley's words were barely inflected and as always her demeanor was unreadable. Which Felix now read, after some experience of her, as an index of her true absence of feeling. Still, this way of speaking signaled something important, though Fe-

lix had no means of knowing what, other than simple malice and a shrewd realism. Despite what she
knew, which was only gossip after all, she really
knew nothing. Not a here-and-now nothing. A
cosmic nothing. She knew that much, and was contemptuous of anyone who thought they knew
more, or could know more, like this inquisitive futile little gnome. It was a judgment.

And for the time being he didn't care. The
waiter brought two full glasses and Felix left them
both to her.

On the way home he stopped at his office and,
coming out, was mugged in the parking lot. They
took his car and a manila envelope.

The Bar

The next morning the police arrived.

It was a woman. She had salty hair and looked
about fifty, though it was hard to tell in someone
so slim and hard. Holstered pistol, handcuffs and
radio behind, but no leather jacket in this weather.
She looked like a motor or a beat cop.

Someone else was here last time, Felix said.

There are several of us.

There's only one of me.

That's why you're hard to find, I guess. You
haven't been to your office.

There's no work. Charles was the one who
brought in the work.

OK. Shall I come in?

You shall, Felix said, opening the door a crack wider.

Just wide enough. She slipped through like a quail under a jojoba bush.

ID, he said. It was out in an instant, a card trick. Sargent Vachon it said. He challenged her. Where's the lieutenant?

Lieutenants are in short supply. Can't afford them.

How long have you been a cop, Sargent? Vachon, Felix added with hasty deference.

Since I was in cop school.

And what were you before? Felix still had his hand on the doorknob.

We're going to go in and sit down now, said Sargent Vachon. You're letting out all the cool air.

Sure, Felix said. Water?

Please.

Never enough water, she said, drinking down what he brought and setting the plastic tumbler aside on Felix's grocery-store end table. Then she settled carefully on the rose brocade sofa and leaned forward, forearms on her knees. Felix saw the strength in her arms. He scooted a chair forward.

This is about Charles? he said.

Yes, it is. And about some other things.

Well, about Charles, then. It's not every day someone gets chloroformed.

It's positively baroque, said Sargent Vachon.

Felix settled on her a speculative eye.

You've been looking into it yourself, she added opaquely.

We were in business. I'm a lawyer. Lawyers have a historic right to look into these things since Perry Mason at least.

And what, then, have you found out, Mr. Kurz? she said, carefully adding the period after his title, abbreviated like himself. Damn all.

Let's hear it.

Charles was said to be — to have been implicated in some, ahh, swindle, though that is disputed.

By who?

A woman named Ashley Portland. She knew these people.

What people.

Through the art gallery Sisters, where she used to work, Gordon Brisbane, and through him Allan Floyd, who funded it after Mona Magdalena died. Through Floyd, his wife Hanna, who died under mysterious circumstances, and through her, her doctoral student Domenic Parra, and through Parra, his friend Fedya Volkoff. Again through Brisbane, the man who succeeded him in funding the gallery, Theodore Makros — known as Dido — and his companion Karen McAdoo, also known through their common practice as potters.

Not quite a comprehensive list, I think, said Sargent Vachon with a wry smile.

Yes, Felix admitted. There is another group of actors with an uncertain relationship to the other.

Through Fedya Volkoff, Ashley came to learn of Connie Anker and through her, her business partner, known initially to us as Constanze Lourdes. Constanze she recognized as a former University student known as Lindsey, her last name uncertain, easily discoverable, and irrelevant. Through Constanze, Ashley came to learn of my assistant Charles, and through him, of me. Through Connie he also came to learn of an accountant in state government, one Chas, and possibly through him, of Allan Floyd by a different route. The connection with Floyd led to his early companion Marta. Allan also forms a possible link between the two groups of actors, and the nexus by which Ashley discovered the nature of Connie Anker's business. This business, originally an arrangement between herself and Chas, came to include Allan and Fedya, as well as Constanze and eventually Charles.

Succinct, Vachon commented. This Ashley Portland seems to have known a great many people. Unusual?

She is a blackmailer. Or rather, one by instinct, currently an apprentice. She had worked actively against Constanze — condition and identity presently unknown, and may have made overtures to others, perhaps thereby setting events in motion and invoking through Charles's death the Detective — that's you — to discover the truth and set things right.

And you, Mr. Kurz?

An accidental corollary, an amateur who was not expected to insert himself into these events. An inconvenience. A cripple who could be counted on to behave as such do, stand aside and observe the workings of a human society of which they are not a part.

Rather in the way we study dolphins or chimpanzees?

Exactly.

Good. Now then, as a student of this alien culture, Mr. Felix Kurz, what construction do you put on the agency of the various characters in the story? On the distribution of knowledge, guilt, responsibility, bad faith, and existential embedding?

Startled, Felix stared.

What about, she went on, this persistent rumor of scam or a conspiracy concerning the valuation of the gallery's holdings?

Felix dismissed this as a baroque fantasy.

How then do you explain the death of Hanna Floyd?

I don't explain it. What do the police know about that?

I wouldn't say, said Sargent Vachon.

Why was there no autopsy? Or if there was, why are the results apparently a state secret?

I wouldn't say.

You and Bartleby.

This allusion did not trouble her in the least. She merely leaned more deeply forward on her forearms, causing the muscles to stand out in her shoulders and neck.

Have you snagged any of these people, Sargent?

Anker. She's left the country. Gone to ground. All in good time. Chas, of course. Fedya is still with us, provisionally. Allan Floyd's fate is also, as you say, apparently a state secret. Constanze Lourdes is dead, probably a suicide.

Probably?

She hung herself. But sometime after that someone released her body, stripped it, and left it discarded on the edge of her bed. We imagine there are people who had an interest in her silence. Considering what harm her knowledge of wealthy powerful men might do. Your Ashley Portland is somewhat at risk now also, I would think.

And Fedya?

The indispensable mechanic in the engine room. Without any firm knowledge of recent events, that is subsequent to Allan's disappearance, we have nothing to go on. We're waiting for him to reveal himself, shall I say?

A mushroom.

Rather a nice image, Felix, given what we know of him.

What do we know of any of them, Felix said irascibly.

Metaphysical question, sir. Can you answer it?

No.

The two of them looked at each other across

an increasingly tense and narrowing gap. Felix was used to such confrontations. So, apparently, was Sargent Vachon

I'm not telling you anything you don't already know, Sargent, he said.

You are not, the Sargent affirmed.

My own idea is, Felix said, though it was in fact not his, is that this is all an invention. You put — that is, two things happen, one after another. We want there to be an explanation, a cause. One thing after another we don't like. Hanna Floyd is dead and no one knows why. Her husband has vanished, leaving behind some unfounded suspicions that no one seems able to confirm, in part because anyone who might confirm them is also dead or vanished, or both. That's six deaths and disappearances, two of which are pretty clearly murders. Quite a lot, and all traceable to the Magdalena Gallery, which is itself vaporware.

Virtual, Vachon said, correcting him.

It's a plague of nothingness. People don't like that. It's the origin of most of the world's religions.

Who are you counting among the murdered? Mr Kurz.

Everyone, physically or spiritually, who was not dead already.

A convenient hypothesis, Felix. I like the baseless fabric of this vision. I like the cloud-capped towers, the gorgeous palaces, the solemn temples. And best of all, the whole insubstantial

pageant, wont to fade away, leaving nothing behind, closing the case, putting us detectives out to
retirement with the bees and vegetable marrows.

Prospero's speech, Felix said.

Hmm?

At the end of *The Tempest*, when he releases
his powers.

Ah. Is it? Something I learned in school, I
suppose.

Felix decided to ignore the Sargent's heavy
irony. Her shift to the familiarity of first names
was an asymmetric move of the same sort, since
Felix did not know her name.

The one thing which is really in need of explanation, she went on, is Charles's death. Aside
from its being a murder for which public order
demands an explanation, if we knew why he is
dead — aside from the fact that most people are —
we might learn something from that about whether
things really are woven together in that way or
whether this is —

An illusion, as I say.

As you say.

An invention. But then, police and lawyers are
in the story-telling business, would you say? An
ancient and noble calling.

Felix was thinking it bizarre to be having this
conversation with a motorcycle cop, a person who
might find such a sensibility not to her benefit
among her colleagues.

Sargent Vachon suddenly loosed her tension

and stood up.

I take it, she said, that's all you know.

Yes.

In that case, I'd like some coffee, she said, holding out the mug now empty of water. Would that be possible?

I'll make a pot.

The Sargent settled herself on a bar stool, ticking off the points, her finger tapping on the gray formica with every item she listed.

There is also the question, Felix, of what you learned from Charles's files which might have caused them to be whisked away. But let's start with Charles. Chloroformed.

Felix nodded with visible satisfaction. I now know something about that, he said.

The double-leaved wooden door of the deceased Mona Magdalena's house in Cave Creek was deeply carved in a vaguely Anasazi motif of inter-locking squares. In one of the panels was a small sign identifying the Magdalena Gallery. Below that was now a second, even smaller sign, newly carved in the same pattern, which read 'Gordon Brisbane' and nothing more.

There was a knocker, somewhat out of Felix's reach. Going to start carrying a cane, he grumbled, stretching upward. The heavy chunk of bronze fell against its striker plate with an inadequate clink. He was about to try it again when the door opened.

Marta.

But you see, Marta said when she brought two cups of coffee to a little table in a corner of the polished stone reception room, under a large red painting which reminded Felix of nothing whatsoever — you see, she said, it's only Gordon and I who are here, and he's not going to answer the door. Besides which, he's gone most of the time. You needn't have knocked. Doors like that are supposed to have knockers, aren't they? It's the security camera which tells me someone is there. Although for you it should be aimed a little lower.

Felix was startled by this frank acknowledgment of his stature. Everyone overlooked that, as automatically as the camera, though perhaps the camera was not embarrassed about it. Over it. One never knows. But he said instead: Gordon is gone where?

Marta shrugged. Talking to artists. Big ones, little ones. Developing the trade. Los Angeles. Wherever there's someone to talk to. Gordon talks well. Don't you think?

No, Felix said. He's supercilious. Full of himself.

Is he? I don't think I know what that means. It's not a word the people who come here use.

What do they use?

Darling.

These are buyers?

You're letting in the flies, Marta said.

Felix scooted his chair back and, apologizing, rose to go. But Marta restrained him with a hand on his arm. Her fingers were stubby, but delicate and cool against his skin. He shuddered, paused, looked again at her black eyes, liquid not with moisture but something like glycerine. The two of them stood together awkwardly a long time. She had caught Felix leaving, his feet one way and his upper body the other, twisted, turned back. Marta was poised on the ball of her back foot, leaning in, preventing his retreat.

Felix shook himself to break the spell.

Come back to the kitchen, Marta said, her voice not entirely kind. I want something to eat. I missed lunch. Are you hungry? I think you said your partner — no, your associate — is dead. My condolences.

He was murdered, Felix said.

Marta hesitated, so that Felix almost collided with her.

Murdered how, she asked, in the kitchen. The coffee grinder prevented Felix from answering, and then the hissing of the espresso machine.

Expensive machine, Felix remarked.

Some of the buyers want it. Espresso. she said with emphasis.

There's something else?

Marta let a little time pass, and then asked about Charles's death.

Chloroform, Felix said. I don't understand.

Chloroform is used in the sex trade, she said after musing on the question for a bit. Child porn. To sedate them, and it makes them forget.

Charles wasn't exactly a child. In some ways, perhaps.

Don't be obtuse, Felix. People don't keep a bottle of chloroform under the sink. There isn't much use for it. You could sniff it. It's in white-out I think. Awfully easy to overdose.

She put down the cup of espresso in front of Felix. No rattly saucer. It clinked lightly on the granite counter-top. Then she made one for herself while Felix pondered Marta's information.

You haven't asked me how I know, she said when the machine's squalling was done. She poured the espresso into a mug which she filled with hot coffee from the filter pot.

I didn't think it would be a good idea, Felix admitted.

You were right.

A long silence passed between them, thinning into friendliness toward the tail end.

Don't sip it, Felix. Two swallows.

And again she laid on finger against his wrist. The unfamiliar touch made Felix quail. Marta felt it, raised an eyebrow, a mere twitch.

So you're saying that Charles was making child porn? Ridiculous.

Is it? No, what I am saying is that if you're a prostitute, if you make videos or act in them, sex shows, whatever, there will be people around who do in fact keep a bottle of it under the sink. I'm saying that it's likely some whore gave it to her.

To Constanze.

Marta shrugged. What do you know about her?

Very little, Felix admitted.

Someone in the sex trade?

Possibly.

So then Charles?

The conversation stopped while Felix assimilated this new idea of who Charles might be. Marta was waiting.

How's the gallery? he managed to ask.

Gordon wants to move it. Have a storefront. Legs traffic, he says. People who will buy the artists he's bringing in are not going to drive up here, he says.

Where to, then?

I don't know. He's looking out for a place. He says. Dido is financing it, of course. Plus what they get out of this two million dollar wreck.

Felix couldn't think of anything to say. Now he wanted to be gone but Marta kept him back, always with a soft touch on the back of his hand, a little brushing of his arm.

On his way back into the city Felix realized that whatever he had observed of Charles was very little and entirely misinterpreted. Several times he pounded the steering wheel with the heel of his hand, and once jammed the brakes so hard he almost caused a rear-ender. The victim blared around Felix, saw what he thought was a child driving, took off with a screech and almost got caught in the cross-traffic at the 101 freeway entrance.

This calmed Felix down.

Sargent Vachon had listened to this tale without a trace of amusement. So your car's been stolen, she said, as if that were the most important thing.

I didn't report that.

Nevertheless, it has. Been stolen. I'm here to get the particulars.

Of what?

The Sargent indicated Felix's dressing gown, bare feet, unkempt hair and unshaven beard. Would you care to dress? I can wait.

No, Felix said sourly. As sour as his mouth. The tilted room had righted itself. No, I wouldn't care to dress. They took a manila envelope.

Who did?

The people who took the envelope. I had found something, but didn't yet know what it was.

And what was in the manila envelope? the Sargent asked.

I don't know, Felix said. The Sargent raised an eyebrow.

They were some notes Charles made on legal pads which I thought might be helpful.

A pause. They both waited for it to melt.

The thing is, Felix said slowly, these notes were in a box of papers in the closet of a room which has nothing else in it, and could hardly be overlooked. And they weren't overlooked. Someone had stirred them up pretty thoroughly. Now if you were looking for case notes or a journal or something, a yellow legal pad would be hard to overlook. Yet it was still there. It wasn't interesting until I found it. Why should that be?

Sargent Vachon held his eye in a new silence for a long while. Then she said again — Helpful to what?

While she waited, the Sargent took a swallow of coffee, then another. Better than mine, she said. Yes?

Felix took a slow breath. There is — or was — a woman Charles was involved with, he admitted. She went by the name of Constanze Lourdes. With another woman, she operated a so-called maid service for wealthy men, some women. For some reason, Charles felt she was — hmm — misrepresenting herself. He'd looked into it. I found the notes.

Regarding the sex trade?

Possibly. It would explain the rather implausible photographs Chas had, and Connie's fear of having her livelihood known. Otherwise extreme. That leaves the question of how Chas came to have them in the first place.

And Charles had looked into this.

Someone had been through the box already. There seemed to be pages missing. I was going to read the rest of them at home to try to work out what. Why they were missing. Why the rest of it was not missing. Unlike what I had thought, that whoever looked through the papers before me had not known what they were looking for. Obviously they had. Very exactly known. Which was why what I did have was stolen, not that it was valuable but because it was not. Or net yet. A sort of plaster cast from which the foot might be known.

Had Charles come to any conclusions?

Not that I could see. Who is Linda Stein?

A high-end prostitute, the Sargent said.

Who was pimping her?

Sargent Vachon ignored this question. When she remade herself as Constanze, the Sargent said, she might have thought she was going to go straight. If so, she could have chosen a better line of work than to clean house for some of the same men who had used her before.

There was something more to it, then.

Probably.

Felix began to pace the room, something he hadn't done since law school, building a defense with other students, students who would refuse to work with him later.

Which would account for she of the many names, he speculated. It could have been Allan Floyd.

The Sargent shrugged.

Well, Felix went on, you don't get to charge those fees out of nowhere.

Some small timers, the Sargent said. Groomed her, sold her to Mr. Floyd.

Again the meticulous titular period.

Charles.

Not known, the Sargent said. I was hoping you might know. So these people, the Connies, built a reputation through sex shows and then mid-level clients. Perhaps the mob moved in before they were ready to cash in their winnings.

Fast rise.

You're not young long, the Sargent replied quietly.

Hangs together, Felix said. I don't like things which hang together like that.

Hmm.

Leaves only Volkoff and Hanna Floyd unaccounted for.

Volkoff, the Sargent said, will lamb it with Connie. He got her out, he can do for himself.

But he didn't know her, Felix protested.

After a while he did.

A pretty short while.

Sargent Vachon shrugged. A triviality, she said.

And so what happened to Hanna Floyd?

Unknown. That will provide the loose end you want, will it?

Felix glared.

We found your car, the Sargent said as she was leaving. In the river bed. Not much wrong with it that wasn't wrong before. You can claim it.

Good of you.

We'll begin again sometime, Felix. Go over the evidence. Speculate. Look for some way to muddy the waters. We can do that, I think.

A motor's bark, a deep fading rumble, and then nothing. Felix got up to shut the door.

Keeps out the flies, he said to himself.

Ashore

So, sayeth Felix Kurz to himself, there remain Powers which are not yet satisfied. Information remains — information which might age, or mould, into knowledge — which has not yet disappeared, been erased, discredited. That which may be found in manila envelopes, particularly. Felix Kurz himself, Caliban of this island, sired by a wizard, taught by magicians, he of dark mien and thick unspeaking tongue, creature himself of the Dark and so not to be disapparitioned from it, nor either from the Light. The Detective, given over to the quest.

It was a plausible story, this business of the two Connies. The best thing about it was the explanation of the chloroform. In fact, it seemed to have been built expressly to explain that one oddity. But it had the same artificiality that Charles's authentication racket had had. Hanna Floyd died. A simple matter goes unexplained. Her husband is a secretive, unpleasant person — the likely culprit therefor. Being guilty, he must be guilty of something. The common fault of both these stories was their need to explain things. Rather than wait for things to explain themselves. Their haste in turning experience into evidence.

Felix thought it not worthwhile to pursue whoever had knocked him down in the parking lot. They, that person, had in the end gotten nothing Felix did not now already have. The police, if they were interested, if that very odd two-cylinder Sargent who probably weighed half her back wheel were interested, they could do what he could not. Felix turned his attention to the other Connie, Anker to her business partner's Lourdes née Stein née Davis. Hilliard. Can she have been ignorant of the use being made of their wealthy clients? The question which had long nagged him, of why she had consented to those photographs Chas made, now had a more plausible answer than the hidden camera ruse. On the other hand, the revenge taken for some sort of betrayal, the rather extreme form of it — she had opened his belly from bottom to top with a quite unusual strength — belied what was probably only a little amateur money laundering for an ad hoc syndicate of three. She had to have known that Chas was not the man she wanted. He might have made the pictures but he didn't out them. Why destroy him, perhaps her only means of finding out who had? Mere anger? That was not consistent with the developing picture of her as a calculating whore.

And then there was Ashley Portland, who seemingly had done what Connie did not, and a much less attractive person all around, a more satisfying murderer certainly, except that the moving finger usually points out the innocent.

The death of Hanna Floyd would probably never be explained. Felix's guess was that Allan's puppeteers — for by that time that's what he surely was, a puppet — had not whisked her away as an inconvenience, a wifeish pothole. Tightly wound as she was, she had probably died of a heart attack, her death in flagrante, in the middle of putting on her stockings, a very ordinary death ignored by everyone. A lesson, in fact, concerning the true nature of human life.

And so a lesson learned in death about the meaning of all this. A black hole of meaning. The death of Hanna Floyd might after all lie at the center of the mystery.

If the chain of inferences behind Felix's conclusions were valid then the circle was closed. A few small-time crooks in over their heads, one murdered, the rest fled, some shenanigans with a bad poet and a forlorn student of exotic religious practices, and an illusory connection to an art gallery manufactured, probably innocently, by the unfathomable Charles, which he had not been able to separate from the truth.

What could be said for Charles? That he was a naïve idealist? None of these people were creatures of the enlightenment. They were poor cleft roots dragged from the soil and tossed aside to moulder back — not tossed, by no one tossed, nor god nor man — or woman — but like fish, perhaps, thrown up on a beach by a storm before their kind had learned to walk. Skitter might be a better word. A wad of people sans feck.

On the shore of his island, where no succor was to be found. From which all Ariel had evaporated and Prospero unprospered, leaving only himself — twisted, angry, bestial, mad, vengeful, untutored indeed ignorant.

Two murders, then. There are always two, the second providing entrée to the first. If Constanze had not stupidly done away with Charles the whole business would have come to lie on the sofa like a sleeping invalid — or rather on the bed wearing one stocking. What was past would have remained in the past, as conjectural as the past always is.

As it was, Felix Kurz — he of the self-contradictory name — was he satisfied with his own deconstruction of the situation which he had been handed and of which he had said falsely from the beginning that he wanted no part of? Was he content to leave it to the police to read what he had written and interpret how they would?

No.

Would he, despite?

Yes.

Gordon Brisbane, with help from Dido Makros's money and property, had succeeded in moving the Magdalena gallery to midtown, on First Street just off Roosevelt, prime space for the artists who he wished to develop. The gallery, now called Brisbane and Makros, was actually a modest space, a white wooden building of about a thousand square feet, large enough to form one gallery plus an entry in which the flasher pieces could be hung, visible to the street through generous windows, and where generous Marta West could have a desk. Marta's business was to greet visitors, explain the artists, hand out price sheets and answer questions about the system of colored dots in use. When not being decorative, she kept the books and managed the inventory. Gordon, who was seldom present, spent his time in studios and places where artists, mostly painters, could be found, in Los Angeles and San Francisco, occasionally raiding farther north. From one of these trips, lasting often months, he returned in company with a large man who proved to be an old companion, Kurt, unearthed in San Diego working for a construction company. But after that sole appearance no one at the First Street gallery saw any more of Kurt, who understandably preferred to travel and so disappeared from this small pool of stagnant evaporating water which was the residue of a vast ocean. As for Dido, he spent much of his time in the gallery. He was knowledgeable and could talk easily to buyers and casual visitors both. Dido's partnership provided Karen McAdoo with a permanent corner in the gallery for her pots, which were priced modestly and sold steadily.

Finally, there was Felix. He hung about like a pariah dog, as if he had nothing to do. Which was true. He had given up his legal aid practice, which never provided a living. It had needed donors, benefactors, people who believed that Kurz would be able to accomplish something positive, however small and local. These had dried up. Felix had gone back to the old hand-to-mouth way of life of earlier days in Guadalupe. He gave legal advice, mostly to people who could pay him only with barter — some tortillas, tamales. menudo, a shirt, plumbing repairs. He got about by bus or borrowed rides. Or he walked. No longer did he care about the time it took. He put on a straw hat with an eight-inch brim, the gift of a man who made them, and carried a bottle of water, and wore a white shirt with tails down to his knees and cut-off jeans and espadrilles, and so attired and provisioned he set out. After a year this life had become comfortable, even necessary. He was the local eccentric, fitted tightly into a crack in the community.

He was even an advertisement of sorts for the gallery, like one of the old signboards. Take a left off Central to First — it's at the Sign of the Dwarf. He was also the gallery's unofficial representative in matters of law, accounting practice, taxes, and general business advice for which Dido paid him a small retainer even though he rarely took the advice. This extra money provided Felix with a bit of dignity by freeing him from a need for handouts.

Felix was sometimes asked for advice or help with other matters — locating runaways, break-ins, shootings, matters of public and domestic order. His practice in these things was not to capture the truth of the matter. He had learned that if he got his hands on anything which looked like truth it would prove otherwise and seep away between his stubby, heavy-knuckled fingers. He solved nothing. He said as little about it as possible, conveying his suggestions through remarks on other things, gesture, apparently irrelevant advice. Talking about the problem, he had discovered, closes possibilities. He solved nothing. To solve is to capture. The truth lives only in open spaces like a feral cat. Felix invited it, gave it room. Matters solved themselves. He spent his time, let secrets reveal themselves. He was a means, a brush for others to paint with.

And so they all scraped along together.

Marta shrugged again. Might be, she said. She lifted her mug an inch off the saucer and set it down again. Men whose hats are too high and bellies are too wide, skinny-ankled women in wired-up underwear.

Marta's moue was half-amused. We talk, she said. We sit in the corner with cups of coffee. This corner. We walk about and make little humming noises in front of mysterious red paintings. I give them Gordon's card with the website address. They go. I go back to what I was doing.

Which was?

Nothing. Playing solitaire.

Boring?

Very much so. It's a living. It's what I do — sit around alone in men's houses keeping them clean of boredom. Attracting all the boredom.

Then when I go to bed at night I barf it all up into the toilet like a mother bird feeding her chicks.

Felix stared at Marta in astonishment. Her bitter words were not said bitterly at all, but with a light amusement, taking innocent pleasure in her own cleverness.

Now, she said, about to go on, but instead took a mouthful of lukewarm coffee. Over the rim of the mug she returned Felix's gaze with an expression which Felix found hard to read. Pensive, but at the same time calculating. She had large black eyes liable to glisten with suppressed emotion. Glistenable.

Now, she said again. This is a twisted business. You're a twisted little man. Probably your mind is as gnarly and stunted as your body. What do you suppose?

Suppose what?

Marta sniggered politely.

Felix was shaken speechless. No one, not even Charles, had ever spoken to him in this way. And yet she seemed not to grant any importance to her words, as if she had taken one too many tranquilizers. She was certainly not now as she had been on Felix's previous visits.

Ahem, he said ostentatiously. I came out to ask about a woman — but his courage failed, and the name of Marta went unspoken.

Should I know her?

Well, yes. It's said —

Who says?

He came across Ashley Portland on a bus. She was dressed in a suit and heels, her hair in tight curls and carrying a valise. Felix knew what was in the valise. Sandwiches.

He never saw her again.

And the time came finally when he went to the gallery on First Street and found it closed, empty. Picked up and moved to Los Angeles. Makros's house in the hands of a caretaker. Karen's studio rented out as a co-op.

It Begins

Felix Kurz stood outside on the street looking in. He took a long drink from his water bottle. He turned and went home again.